Darkened

A Novel

Daniel Sacketos

Printed in the United States of America
First Printing, 2020
ISBN 978-1-951824-01-3

D.A.S Book Publishing
Dasbookpub@gmail.com

Thank you *Jason* for being my mentor, teaching me of fine wine, and wanting to go into that book store that day.

Thank you *Taylor* for helping me piece this together, being you, and being my rock.

Thank you *Regina*

Thank you to my *family* and *friends* who have unknowingly helped me on this journey.

Darkened

having no light; made dark.

1

IDA

I da ran quickly through the murky forest, with twigs and thorns tearing into the soles of her bare feet. All around her, cries of "Witch!" rang out, but the young girl didn't stop until she came across a small creek in the woods. A quick snap of a branch caught her attention, coming to an imitate stop, ahead of her was a deer, with soulless dark eyes staring at her. With her heart in her mouth, Ida hesitated to consider what to do next. Unbeknownst to her, a pair of eyes red with rage had locked on her from behind, with the person's arms stretched forward, holding a metal that glistened under the moonlight.

A loud, booming noise rang through the forest, but Ida was a second late to hear it as a bullet from the rifle hit her in the shoulder. Ida lurched forward and fell to the ground. She could hear a man yelling, "The witch! I shot the witch!" At that moment, Ida knew it was nearly over for her. Panicking, she began to crawl through the dirt and dead leaves on the ground. There was only one thought on her mind—survival.

Ida put all her strength into crawling out of the woods, but she hadn't gone far before the townspeople had caught up to her. "Witch," an old woman had yelled while her heavily-bearded husband kicked Ida in the stomach, sending her flipping on her back as she spurted crimson-red blood from the corner of her mouth. Another man grabbed Ida by her hair, pulling forcefully as he reeled her up on her feet. The young girl cried out in pain. "Spawn of Satan," the man called her as he pulled her hair with more force. His wife edged him on, saying, "We must cleanse the witch." "Yes, we must burn the witch," a voice of a younger man stated with conviction.

Ida had recognized the voice; it was that of Mr. Cameron, a gentle-looking man who headed the town's youth group. To Ida's utmost shock and horror, she saw Mr. Cameron grab an already knotted noose and throw the rope over a tree while another young man began to pour a liquid onto the tree. It had the unmistakable smell of oil.

Ida pleaded for them to stop. In response, a woman smacked her face with the back of her hand. Ida looked at her with pure contempt. Seeing the hateful look on her face, the crowd began their witch chant louder. Meanwhile, Mr. Cameron ordered some of the young men to tie her hands behind her as he placed the noose around her neck. He began to pull the rope up.

The women in the crowd cheered on the scene, shouting "Yes! Yes!" Meanwhile, Ida desperately gasped for air as she tried to use her legs to break free. This futile attempt to escape elicited laughter from the women as they jeered at her. One shouted over the noise, "Quickly cleanse the soul, burn the witch! Burn the witch!" Picking up on this, the crowd began to chant incessantly, "Burn the witch! Burn the witch! Burn the witch!"

Just then, Mr. Cameron picked up a flaming torch and lit the fire below the girl's feet. In little time, the flames began to intensify as it licked the edges of Ida's white gown, which had now turned the color of mud and earth. Suppressed cries came from Ida's throat, pleading and wailing for her innocence. She wanted it to be over. The townspeople cheered aloud as the fire began consuming the flesh on the girl's body. In her last bid for solace, Ida turned her eyes to the sky, the blue in them reaching out to match that in the sky above. She smiled one last time at the beautiful stars that graced the night sky, oblivious to the horror men were wreaking below. At that moment, the light in Ida's eyes went out, and everything turned black as she let out one final, blood-curdling scream.

⁓

The birds chirped heartily as they flew past above the deserted road.

Danny usually enjoyed the serene atmosphere and the calmness the birds' music gave him. However, on that day, he was much preoccupied with the task before him.

Danny was hanging from a tree above a ditch, attempting to tie a rope around the grill of an old car. Once balanced, he began to pull the knot tight slowly, methodically as if he had done it a hundred times before. He tugged at the rope, and the silver bumper began to rip slowly.

Danny climbed down from the tree, slung the rope over his shoulder, and like a hunter, began hauling his catch—which rather than being game, was a spare part from a dingy, old car. The load seemed a bit heavy for his twenty-year-old arms, but Danny considered activities like this as a free, unorthodox workout. As he exited the forest, sweat dripped down from his face to his clothes and body but he made no attempt to wipe it off. The sun wasn't high yet in the sky, but even then, the summer heat was intense enough.

Danny hopped on his dirt bike and began driving down the road.

A few minutes later, he pulled up in front of his house: a rundown mobile home surrounded by forest. Danny released the kickstand on his bike, and he tossed the bumper on a pile of sliver parts.

A large Doberman appeared out of nowhere, catching Danny off-guard as he jumped at him. Danny took a step back and knelt to pat the dog's head. "Easy, Zeus. I guess you've missed me, boy," Danny said.

In response, Zeus began sniffing the air as he tried to get closer to the bag Danny held in his hand. Sensing the dog's instinct, Danny reached into his bag and hauled out a piece of dried jerky. He signaled to Zeus to sit and then he dropped the jerky in front of him.

Leaving the dog to tackle his meal, Danny stood up and headed into the house. The door creaked noisily as he closed it behind him. Inside was dark and messy. On an ancient couch sat a man with matted, long hair and a messy, brown beard. The man was close to sixty years of age but one would've guessed that he was at least a decade older. He snored loudly, with a beer can gripped in his hand while others lay scattered on the floor all around him. His eyes were screwed shut tightly, oblivious of his son. The fuzzy TV before him was turned on to the local sports channel.

Danny sighed as he stared at his father, pausing for a moment as he watched the man lying perfectly still; he wondered if he was breathing. Just then, the old man belched in his sleep and began scratching his scrawny beard.

Danny shook his head and slowly made his way to his room, wondering how he was related to that pathetic, old man.

In his room, he took off his soiled shirt and flung it aside. Standing in front of a wall mirror, he observed his lean muscular body. He looked like garbage, he admitted. His eyes roved to a photo clipped above the mirror. The picture was of a woman smiling, holding a beer can, wearing an oversized leather jacket. Danny admired the photo as he quickly banished the thoughts running through his mind before they overwhelmed him.

Danny pulled on a pair of his clean work clothes and went to the backyard. For his morning training regimen, he climbed a dirty rope tied to a tall tree while Zeus stared at him from below.

After climbing up and down a few times, Danny picked up an axe and began chopping wood. Ten minutes later, he glanced at an old clock above the garage door; it was 8:15 am already.

Danny quickly rushed inside to freshen up. Five minutes later, he was riding off to school. Zeus ran after the bike for a while but when the machine picked up momentum, the dog knew he couldn't keep up anymore so he stopped and turned back home.

The bell rang aloud.

Danny navigated through the horde of students in the hall as he made his way for class. Inside, he sat down and pulled out his pencil and notebook. His classmates were beginning to rush in, taking their seats all around him.

Gill, a tall, chubby boy with the gait of a beanbag with arms, strutted into the room like he owned the place. He scanned the room with his eyes and, spotting his target, he headed inside and sat behind Danny.

Danny's face went expressionless; he had encountered this jerk several times before, and he was beginning to get tired of his gimmicks.

Gill grinned mischievously as he jolted his desk forward, hitting Danny's chair. He cackled aloud as he slammed the desk against the chair over and over again.

Danny clenched his fists. One more push and he was going to break the guy's jaw, he promised himself.

Just then, a young girl of Danny's age stepped into the class. With a hand holding one strap of her bag, she walked up to Gill and slapped him lightly on the head.

"Stop that, Gillian," the girl stated.

Startled, Gill turned around to see who dared slap his head. Seeing it was Jessica, he smiled coyly, and without a word, he stood up and went to sit with his friends.

The girl then went on to take the seat directly in front of Danny. She glanced back and said, "Hi, Danny."

"Hi, Jessica," he replied, taking in her beauty once again. He always marveled at how effortlessly gorgeous and sophisticated she looked. Coupled with that, Danny found her to be the most relatable person in the classroom, and for that reason, he made her his friend.

Jessica caught him looking at her face for too long; colors flushed to her cheeks and she quickly tried to hide her blush by changing the topic. "Looks like Mrs. Hork is running late again," she said as she opened her bag and handed Danny her book with their homework.

"Thanks," replied Danny. He quickly flipped through the book and began copying the answers to their homework. He noticed Jessica was watching him. "I know. I know. I owe you," he said without taking his eyes off the answers he was copying.

Jessica disregarded his explanation casually. Instead, she asked, "What do you want to do?"

"What do you mean?"

Jessica rephrased her question. "What would you like to do in life? Like forever." "Well, I want to get out of this town," he responded.

Just then, Mrs. Hork entered the classroom, walking with elegance in her heels as they click-clacked against the floor. Her application form indicated that she was in her late thirties. However, the woman still dressed and acted like a much younger woman, as if in denial that the years had passed on her.

"Sorry I'm late, class! Car troubles, but God is good! Remember that," she said as she walked up to the front of the class.

Danny shot Jessica a knowing look, and they both giggled as she quickly turned to look forward. Smiling, she stretched her hand behind her back and Danny placed the homework in her palm.

Just then, someone shouted, "Danny's cheating!"

Danny's eyes quickly darted around the classroom, and unsurprisingly, he discovered it was Gill who had snitched on him.

Mrs. Hork stopped her incessant rant and held the chalk stick to the board, unmoving.

She paused for a moment before stomping her heels down as she made her way toward Danny.

Danny turned his head down, waiting.

The teacher approached. "Cheating... Who do you think you are?" She got down to Danny's level, almost face to face. "Especially after what your father did to this town. Spawn of Satan."

Danny was drowning in embarrassment, and he felt like disappearing. His jaws clenched as he drove his rage toward getting revenge on Gill.

Mrs. Hork snatched his homework from the table and scribbled something onto it furiously. "F!" she yelled before throwing the paper at him.

As the teacher stomped off, Jessica looked at Danny with concern. *Thank God it's over now*, Danny thought as he raised his head and winked at Jessica.

***

Danny sat on a bench inside the school's cafeteria, eating his lunch. Sitting across from him was Jessica and a cute, Asian girl named Mikayla. The trio was busy trying to consume their food before the break is over.

However, Danny had an uneasy feeling and the only time he often felt this way was when he was in danger. As he looked up, his dread was confirmed. Approaching him was Keith, a sports jock with dark hair, a square-set jaw, and handsome facial features. Following closely behind was Mitch, a light-haired, blue-eyed guy with a rugged look. If Mitch wasn't in school, he would've probably been a drifter. *Perhaps he could still be*, Danny thought. Walking at the back of the duo was none other than Gill.

As soon as their eyes met, Gill signaled to his crew and pointed at Danny.

He was vastly outnumbered. There were times to prove brave and stand up to assholes, no matter how many they were, but this wasn't one of those times. Not today. Danny grabbed his bag and ran out the other way.

———✥———

Danny made his way through the school hallway with an apple wedged between his teeth. He kept his head down as he rushed through the crowd. Ahead, he saw a policewoman talking to their school principal, Mr. Red. The principal, in his fifties, had a head as hairy as an egg while the woman he was talking to was at most twenty years younger than him. She had her hair tied in a ponytail.

Danny knew the policewoman; her name was Teresa. Their paths had crossed in the past and they had a sort of history. Sighting the woman talking with his principal, Danny had mixed feeling about whether to go say hi to her. He decided otherwise, and he kept his eyes down as he walked past them.

Officer Teresa noticed Danny walking by and since she had rounded up her conservation with the principal already, she patted him on the back and said goodbye. Then she turned around and called out, "Danny."

Danny stopped in his tracks and looked back. "Hi, officer."

The policewoman looked at him compassionately. "How are things?" she asked.

Danny shrugged. "You look nice," he stated instead.

Teresa looked down, blushing warmly. The moment passed.

"I haven't heard from you in a while, Danny. Sure things are okay?" she asked.

Confronted again by the question, Danny replied, "Things are okay, still saving."

Officer Teresa nodded in understanding. She pondered on his words for a moment before responding. "Maybe you should stay. You can try and figure things out." Seeing the determined look in his eyes, the policewoman knew she couldn't change his mind with mere words. She changed the topic by asking, "Are those boys still bothering you?"

"Nothing I can't handle, Teresa," Danny replied, flaunting a fake confident smile. Officer Teresa studied him for a minute as if considering making a decision about him.

Then, she nodded again. "Stop by tonight," she said as she turned around and began walking away without a response.

Danny watched her go and as she turned around a corner, he began backing into the maintenance room, with a smirk on his face.

Inside, the maintenance room looked like an old factory, dimly lit by a fluctuating lamp. A bed was positioned against the far corner wall. Without giving the room a second look, Danny tossed his bag on the floor and sat down.

Just then, the door opened and in walked Jeff. Well, he did more limping than walking. The old man looked so ancient that some students had placed bets on whether the man had been alive during the Roman conquest in the middle ages or since Moses's exodus in ancient Egypt. Although the old man, with his bald head and toothless mouth, looked indeed like something out of the history pages, Danny pegged Jeff's age to be around seventy or eighty.

"Hey, Jeff, what's the word?" Danny asked musingly.

Jeff mumbled with difficulty. "More puke... Fuckers!" he blurted.

Danny laughed and nearly lost his balance at the desk he sat at. He respected the old man. Jeff kept his nose out of his business and never felt the need to prod about how he was feeling, even though he had worked with his mom and was almost a second dad to Danny.

Although the maintenance room wasn't the most lavish hangout, it beat being around his dad at home. Jeff welcomed the company without question, and in return, Danny helped him out with his day-to-day duties. Their silent agreement seemed to work well for the both of them. Jeff also encouraged Danny to finish school, keeping him on the right track after what had happened to his mother. Although, Danny being older than his classmates, Jeff reminded him its what his mother would have wanted.

"Want me to grab it?" Danny asked.

"No, fucker... I got it!" the old man responded.

Danny raised his hands above his head in mock surrender. "Alright, Jeffery, radio me if you need anything."

The old man grunted in response as he headed out of the maintenance room, mumbling. On the desk in front of Danny was a radio. He picked it up and adjusted the dial before jumping onto the rusty bed. He saw a football in a corner and he stretched to pick it up.

Danny tossed the ball at the wall and it bounced back at him. He was elated by the feeling, and he repeated it a few more times. However, at the fifth throw, a newspaper pasted on the wall came undone; it floated in the air for a second, unfolding before the soft wind blew it into Danny's lap. Featured in the newspaper was a picture of his parents. Danny stared at it, hesitantly. Then he reached out his hand and touched the newspaper, resting his finger on his dad's picture. Slowly, he glided the finger over to the picture of his mother.

Emotions began flooding Danny's body, and memories and images ran through his head.

He couldn't deal with that at the moment. By then, it was already dusk.

Danny got up and flicked a few switches. Outside the school premises, the lights went off.

As he made to lie back on the bed, the radio crackled and came to life. "Dan..." a voice called out over the static.

Danny quickly walked over and grabbed the walkie-talkie off the desk. The radio transmission fuzzed.

Danny clicked. "Jeff...?" Nothing. He clicked again. "Hello?" Static.

Danny grabbed a mop bucket from a corner of the room. Slinging his gray uniform jacket over his shoulder, he headed out of the maintenance room.

Dragging the mop bucket on the cold floor, Danny walked down the dark, empty hallways. There was no Jeff in sight. The cool breeze made the air a bit chilly, and Danny considered wearing his jacket. He shrugged off the thought as he made his way toward the school gymnasium.

Danny stuck his head through the door. "Jeff!" He called out. There was no response.

Danny loved the calm atmosphere in the gym at night, compared to the noise and sweaty smell that dominated the room in the daytime. He walked to the middle of the court and picked up a basketball from the rack. He aimed at the hoop and shot; he missed.

Encouraged by his first attempt, he turned around and headed toward the exit door. Just then, a loud noise came from the pool area, and Danny began running in that direction.

Danny rushed in with the mop bucket in hand. The blue hue of the water's reflection bounced off Danny's face. He sighed in relief as he saw there was no one in the pool. Is initial fear was that the old man had slipped and fallen into the water. Knowing that the frail man had no strength to swim, he would've drowned like a bootstrapped pirate. *Thankfully, none of that happened,* he thought.

As he stared at the water, he noticed a shadow creeping up behind him. He turned too late to see Keith's face as he pushed him into the pool.

"Scumbag!" he shouted.

Danny rose in the water slowly. "Asshole!"

Keith was enraged by the remark but he couldn't do anything while Danny was still in the water.

Gill and Mitch stepped out from their hiding place, and they began circling the edge of the pool.

"Why are you talking to my girl, faggot?" Keith said.

Danny was still in the water as he stared at him. He didn't utter a single word. As he played dumb, Keith got more infuriated.

"Gill, get that side," he ordered his friend, gesticulating to where he wanted him to go.

Mitch looked thrilled by the prospect of beating up Danny. "Come here, mommy's boy."

Danny looked around as they circled him; once again, he was outnumbered three to one. Thinking on his feet, he began swimming toward the weakest amongst his adversaries: Mitch. As he got closer, the look of excitement on Mitch's face turned to anger when he saw

Danny dip his palms into the pool, scooped a handful, and splash him with a wave of water.

Mitch was drenched. "You motherfucker!"

Without hesitating, Danny turned sideways and splashed Keith twice in quick succession.

Keith's eyes widened in anger, and he yelled, "My fucking phone! I'm gonna kill you!" Danny chuckled, knowing he had the edge over them as long as he was in the water.

The three bullies tried to circle around him and attack but each time they got closer, Danny splashed them with more water, forcing them to retreat. When they were as nearly drenched as he was, they decided to leave him alone and deal with him in their next encounter.

"Just wait, bitch," Keith threatened as he stepped out of the door.

Gill stood around a little longer, pondering on whether to enter the pool and beat up Danny. However, his decision was made for him as he got splashed with more water. "Fuck!" he remarked as he began rushing out of the room after his friends.

Mitch held up his middle finger up as he followed after his companions. "See you soon, mommy's boy!" he stated.

Danny waited in the pool for a few more minutes to be sure they wouldn't come back. When he was getting out of breath, he slopped himself out of the pool. He began dragging his feet as his clothes had become heavy from the accumulated water.

Danny noticed that noise was coming from behind a closet. As he approached it, he noticed a red pool noodle had been used to tie the door. He loosened it and stepped out of the way just in time to see Jeff pushing the door out with anger.

The old man was mumbling furiously. "Fuckers! Little fuckers!"

Danny couldn't contain his laughter. "You okay?" he asked amid giggles. Jeff eyed him with contempt. "Shut ump!"

Danny busted into laughter as he watched the old man limp off. Danny bent over, cackling. The night had indeed gone much better than he could've hoped for.

<hr />

The laundry machine buzzed loudly, working at a high. However, the two occupants of the room paid it little attention. They were focused on each other, touching and kissing.

Danny's lips came down on Officer Teresa's, kissing her. Gently at first, then more insistently, his tongue demanding entrance. She could taste his sweetness in his kiss.

His chin brushed roughly against her skin. But it was his hands that were on her mind. His hands that were roaming her small body, pulling her into him. She could feel a large bulge forming in his pants, no doubt in her mind what that was. She'd seen it several times before. The thought of the young stud filling her up again was exhilarating. Her breathing was coming faster now.

There were fingers on her neck, fumbling with the buttons on her top. Teresa felt the thin material fall away, exposing her breasts to his hungry gaze. Her nipples became erect, standing out proudly as the cool air of the room brushed her bare breasts.

His fingers pinched her nipples. His tongue. *Oh, God!* Teresa thought. His mouth was on her nipple and it felt so good, she moaned.

Her body shook with a violent spasm, an orgasm building up inside her, her fingers digging into his shoulders. The sheer suddenness of it, surprising her.

Teresa felt a pull on her little zipper, her dress falling completely away, sliding down her slender frame and pooling at her feet. She was naked. Naked in the arms of Danny. Once again, her thoughts were interrupted as his hands gripped her naked ass and pulled her roughly against his hard body, his tongue driving between her lips.

Pulling away from their kiss, he pushed her back at arm's length, his eyes drinking in her naked body. "Take off my pants," he said.

Teresa looked at him blankly, not used to being told what to do, to being ordered.

But she dutifully knelt and began to fumble with the zipper to his pants, her fingers shaking as she reached for his cock. Her fingers traced along the thickening length of that hard rod, touching it gingerly. Almost as if afraid of what was before her eyes.

The heat from it burned her fingers as she tried to wrap them around its girth.

Danny lifted up the police officer and set her up on a washing machine. She spread her legs apart, and Danny pressed her against the wall as he slid his cock deep inside her warm, eager hole.

Teresa gave him a great view of her body as he penetrated her slowly; her glowing, pink butt cheeks creaked against the washing machine as a result of the jerky motion.

Danny worked his hand down to Teresa's hips, feeling out the soft curves as her smooth stomach met her round hips. He spread her legs further apart, her muscles softening as he put his thumb on her clit and rubbed softly. Teresa was ready to come, and Danny wanted to feel her climax from inside her.

Danny could feel himself getting ready to cum, and Teresa was moaning louder with each thrust of his dick inside her. As she grabbed the wall in climax, Danny reached his peak as well, groaning aloud as he came.

Danny heaved aloud as he lay on the floor beside Teresa, reliving their just-concluded sexual escapade. He could only summarize it with one word; fantastic. The woman had seemed out of breath. They stared at each other, smiling sheepishly.

Danny stood up unexpectedly and went over to the drier to retrieve his clothes. He began putting them on.

"Thought you were spending the night," Teresa said.

"Have things to do," Danny stated. He was fully clothed by then. Teresa eyed him affectionately. "Do you ever sleep?" she asked.

Danny leaned in and planted a kiss on her forehead, making her smile. "No," he responded.

He walked out of the laundry room and started heading home.

Spotting his jacket on the floor, Teresa picked it up and smelt it. She felt a tingle in her spine. "I'm keeping your jacket!" she called out after him with the hope of making him come back for another bout of sex. However, Danny was far gone already.

***

It was a full moon that night, and the silver light shone on Danny as he rode his bike home. Trumping Gill and friends and watching Jeff mumble through his toothless mouth in anger had provided him some excitement. However, his time at Teresa's place was thrilling and it left him with a warm glow in his heart.

Upon getting home, Danny went straight to his room. He pulled the curtains and stared out of his window, glaring directly at the moon. For a moment, he imagined that behind that big ball of gas, there were eyes looking back at him.

The moment passed, and Danny turned around. Kicking off his shoes, he fell onto the bed, where Zeus lay cuddled up already. In no time, he drifted off to a pleasant sleep.

The next morning, Danny whistled as he went about his morning chores. The axe made a thumping noise each time he brought it down on a block of wood. Shirtless, his skin glistened with sweat. He continued chopping until he was out of breath. He then placed the handle of the axe against the floor as he rested his head against the cold metal at the top.

Zeus growled angrily, looking at the window. Danny followed his eyesight to see what the noise was about. Unsurprisingly, he saw his father's face at the window, staring at him while he worked. Zeus was a friendly Doberman, but he always seemed agitated by the sight of David. The dog seemed to take a dislike to his father, just like the folks around town.

As Danny's and his father's eyes met, the older man held his gaze for a few seconds before he turned around and disappeared into the darkness of the home.

Danny finished up his chores on time that day and headed for school. In class, he walked in to see that Jessica had already arrived before him. He smiled at her as he took the seat behind her. He couldn't help but stare at her back, shoulders, and lustrous hair as the light bounced off her fair skin. In order to prevent ogling at her, he looked away.

Just then, Jessica quickly turned around. "What are you doing today?" she asked.

"Me?" Danny asked with a puzzled look on his face as he was caught completely off- guard by the question.

"Yeah, you dork," Jessica teased.

"Nothing," Danny replied.

"Want to grab some ice cream like old times?"

Danny pondered it for a moment. Hanging out with Jessica seemed like a great idea. However, he had a slight concern. "What about Keith?"

Jessica smiled coyly. "He's in Florida with Gill and Mitch."

With doubts in his mind, Danny looked around the room; there really was no sign of Gill or his friends. Danny was still unconvinced about being seen together outside with Jessica.

Sensing his hesitation, Jessica tugged at his arm playfully. "Come on. It'll be fun," she pleaded.

Danny saw her bite her lip reflexively, a glaring sign that she was nervous. He was making her nervous about asking him out. Danny dwelled on the thought for a minute and chuckled.

"Just like old times," Jessica said. She pleaded to him in desperation by giving Danny her brightest smile.

He hesitated for a second as he studied her face. He couldn't say no to her smile; no one could. "Fine, double chocolate crunch, extra fudge," he said.

Jessica looked amazed as her eyes grew wild. "Oh my god! How on Earth do you still remember that?"

"Some things you just don't forget," Danny replied.

Jessica nodded affirmatively, impressed by his accurate memory.

2

SHOTGUN

A loud noise rang through the garage of the mobile home. Inside, it wasn't aesthetically appealing— the same as the rest of the house. Danny had lost his sight for decorating and beauty a long time ago, no thanks to his father's bland taste.

At the moment, decorating wasn't what dominated Danny's mind as he reached for the top shelf in the garage and pulled down an old shoebox. He brushed the dust off it as he removed the cover. Scattered inside was junk and memorabilia, including a red and blue thermos.

He retrieved the thermos from the box and opened it. Rolled up inside was a little bundle of dollar bills and coins. Danny emptied out the contents of the thermos and he gathered all the quarters into his pocket. Spotting a photo of his mother amongst the items on the shelf top, Danny smiled and quickly put all the items back in their places.

He locked the garage and got on his bike. He began driving off. He, however, hadn't gone far before something by the side of the dirt path caught his eye. It was a flower, a beautiful, vibrant, red one. *A perfect gift for Jessica*, he thought as he got off his bike.

Danny walked down the side of the road toward the flower. He plucked it, staring at the weird pattern of the petals for a moment. He wondered what type of flower it was. As he looked on, Danny felt a presence behind him, and he turned around quickly. To his surprise, standing closely behind him was a huge deer; Danny was baffled by how quickly the animal had crept up behind him without him noticing.

What was more worrisome about the scene was that the deer was giving him a dead- eyed stare, glaring at him with black, soulless eyes as if he wanted to see beneath his skin. The long antlers on the animal's head were threatening enough.

Danny took a step back, his brain working overtime to find an escape route in case the animal charged at him. Just then, the deer began to breathe heavily, wheezing.

It let out a quick sneeze from his snout before turning around and dashing into the forest.

Danny tried to follow it, but the animal had disappeared amongst the trees as if it had stepped into another dimension. It was puzzling.

Danny had wasted enough time waiting around, and he couldn't afford to go chasing after a deer in the forest. He turned back and got on his bike once again. Kicking off, he revved up the engine and started heading into town, with the red flower attached to the back of the bike.

After riding for about ten minutes, Danny pulled up in front of Jessica's house. The building had a nice, Victorian style design that was uncommon in that part of town.

The front door flung open and out rushed Jessica. She quickly ran up to Danny and embraced him; he returned the gesture. Meanwhile, a man stepped out of the house and stood on the porch, observing them. Danny waved at Jessica's dad, but he got no response in return.

Breaking away from the hug, Jessica hopped on the bike's seat. She wrapped her arms around Danny's stomach. Nervously, she began to say, "I've never been on a motorcycle before, please drive slo—"

Without warning, Danny began accelerating. Jessica bucked where she sat, and she held him tighter. She screamed and hooted, giggling sheepishly as they rode off to town.

The ice cream store was located in a more populated part of town. The store had been around since forever and although the management did a good job of constant renovation, the chipped off paint and weather-beaten roof stood as evidence of just how many decades had passed on the iconic establishment. The small building had a patio outside where people sat and enjoyed their sweet delicacies; many of whom were chatting with one another, while a few loners were relaxed in their seats, enjoying the cool breeze.

Danny and Jessica stood outside the front door as if waiting for an invitation to enter.

Both pairs of their eyes darted around, taking in the time-eroded compound. Memories of their childhood came rushing back to mind, leaving a bittersweet taste of nostalgia in their mouths. Those memories were good ones, Danny admitted to himself.

"Remember when we used to play tag over there," he said, nodding his head toward the left corner wall of the building.

Jessica laughed. "They sure hated us for that."

They both glanced at each other and smiled, it felt like it was another lifetime ago that they were innocent, little kids playing around, skinning their knees, and making pinky swears. Then, they were oblivious to how tumultuous the world really was. As he looked at the pretty, doe-eyed girl he had spent a lot of his childhood with, Danny wished that he could go back to those days. He silently swore that he would give up anything to get another chance to relive those moments. However, the truth was that all he had were wishes, and over the years, he had come to painfully understand that wishful thinking does not help anyone. He had found out that particular essential life lesson at a great price.

Pushing his thoughts aside, Danny opened the door and headed to the register with Jessica beside him. The young man behind the counter who was only about two years older than Danny smiled at them as he waited patiently for their order.

"May I have a small double chocolate crunch, extra fudge," Jessica requested.

As the cashier turned to go get her order, Danny quickly added, "Make that a medium."

Jessica glanced at him, her eyebrow raised quizzically.

"We need to keep the tradition alive," he replied, smirking. "Very well then, I accept the challenge."

Not wanting to make two trips, the cashier stared at Danny, looking to take his order at the same time.

Catching his eye, Danny began shaking his head. "Oh, no. I'm good." Jessica stared at him, unconvinced. "You're not gonna get anything?"

"No, I'm okay. I promise," Danny replied, smiling reassuringly.

Jessica stopped her inquiry. She opened her purse and pulled out a five-dollar bill, which she handed to the cashier. Danny had already planned to pay for her ice cream so he grabbed the money from the cashier and placed it back in Jessica's palm.

"It's on me," he said as he quickly stretched his hand into his trouser pocket.

By then, the cashier had gone to fetch their order and he came back with Jessica's ice cream. "It's $2.25."

Danny pulled out a handful of quarters. They made

a loud rattling noise as he placed them on the table. The sound attracted the attention of a few people around as they glanced at the register. Danny's cheeks flushed with embarrassment. Studying his facial expression, Jessica looked down in an attempt to suppress a giggle.

Danny collected the ice cream from the cashier and gave it to Jessica. He looked up at the older young man once more. "Keep the change," he said, winking.

Jessica and Danny busted into laughter as they headed out of the store and walked to the patio. Locating a vacant bench, they sat down facing each other.

Jessica pulled out her smartphone. She opened an app and stared at the screen. "This app is amazing. It's called Locator," she said.

Danny nodded nonchalantly. "I just don't understand why you would want people to know where you are."

"Well, it's for safety, dummy. See my dad, here. Mikayla too—they can see me," she said, pointing to a small dotted icon on her screen.

Danny made a lackluster attempt to look. After seeing what it was about, he shook his head.

Jessica smiled, saying, "Now you are making me look like the dork here." Danny chuckled. "What about

Keith?" he asked, looking agitated.

Jessica's smile disappeared as she stared at his face. "I don't have him on here."

Sensing his paranoia, she reached out and grabbed his arm. "Relax, Danny," she added in a more pacifying tone.

"I'm relaxed. Really, I'm fine," he replied, forcing a nervous smile.

Jessica rubbed his arm passionately as an idea crossed her mind. "You and I, let's go to the forest before it gets dark. That's only if you're brave enough," she dared.

Danny gave her a skeptical look, wondering if she was joking or not. "Witch's Creek, you mean?"

She nodded.

"Aren't you afraid?" he asked.

Jessica noted the hint of danger in his voice. "I believe it's only a myth," she stated, hesitantly.

Danny scoffed. "No—Yeah. I'm pretty sure it's not a myth."

Jessica looked unconvinced. She wouldn't be deterred from going on an adventure with a friend just because of an old town's folklore. She pestered him on. "Come on. I have you to protect me," she said, giving him puppy-eyes as she smiled coyly.

Once again, Danny was faced with a decision-making

process pertaining to Jessica. However, once again, the tie was decided by the irresistible smile. He couldn't just say no after seeing that set of perfectly-capped, white teeth.

Ten minutes later, they were on the road, barreling down toward the mysterious forest. An old, wooden sign was erected by the side of the road. It was broken, and some of the words written with paint and carvings on it had faded already. The sign now read, "Wit_h_ _reek." The bike blew dust on it as they zoomed past the sign that heralded their welcome to the mysterious forest.

As they reached the end of the tarred road, which stopped where the forest vegetation began, Danny parked his bike. With Jessica by his side, they began walking down the long, cleared path that led to the undergrowth of the huge, tall trees. There was not a single sound coming from the forest, except for the noise their feet made crunching on the leaves. Although birds flew and nested above the tall tree branches, none of them chirped or made any form of sound. It was as if when they entered the forest, they had stepped into a world where the animals lived in silent protest.

As they walked on, Jessica made an attempt to turn the creepy atmosphere down a few notches by starting up a conversation. "Things are so different now, ever since what happened…" Her voice trailed off, as if considering the right words to say next.

"Why does Mrs. Hork hate you so much?" Jessica regretfully asked. Danny hesitated for a moment. "I think she sees a lot of my father in me…" Danny replied. As Danny strutted along, he picked up on it. "That's why I want to leave. It's been hell living in this town, everything here reminds me of her… I've been saving up. Got three grand already now."

Jessica was shocked. "Get out! Where'd you get all that money?"

He shrugged. "I've been saving ever since she passed. Also, selling silver and working at the school."

Astonished by his last statement, Jessica's eyes grew wild as she blurted, "Selling Silver? Wait. Cedarville? Was that you?!"

Danny grinned, raising his hands up in mock surrender. "Guilty."

"Danny! You're so bad!" she said, punching him in the shoulder. "Ow!" Danny screwed up his face as he grabbed his shoulder.

They both roared in laughter, their voices echoing through the woods.

Danny secretly retrieved something from his bag and hid it behind his back while Jessica was distracted. It was the red flower, and he made sure he kept it out of sight; he wanted to surprise her completely.

As he looked up, he saw that Jessica was already making her way ahead as she headed toward a ditch that was separated from the path with a large stone.

"Where are you going?" he called out. She gave him no response. All she did was stare at a giant boulder, her back to him. Danny went after her and grabbed her shoulder, turning her to face him.

Unexpectedly, Jessica lunged forward and placed her lips on his, kissing him. The surprise quickly wore off as Danny kissed her back, leaning in closer as he moved his free hand up to the back of her neck.

Jessica thrust her tongue deep into his mouth without warning. He felt a jolt come from the girl, as though she hadn't had such a sensual kiss in a long time. He gripped her tighter with his fingers and felt her hot, young body press against him. Jessica ran her wet tongue over his lips. The sexual tension was beginning to grow inside Danny, and he intensified their kiss by driving his tongue into her mouth, running it over hers while their lips remained locked in a furious battle. They both moaned in pleasure.

He was excited by how eager she seemed as he felt her body quiver. They parted their lips slightly to catch their breaths but their tongues still remained together in an erotic dance.

Out of nowhere, an unusually loud, mechanical noise echoed through the forest, jolting the two of them back to reality. They let go of each other and turned around to see what the source of the noise was.

As the sound grew closer, they identified the noise as car honks and automobile engine sounds. Sure enough, a pickup truck came into sight, and as it rumbled closer, Danny saw an unmistakable head peering out from the back of the truck; it was Gill's buddy, Mitch, who at that moment opened his mouth and shouted over the sound of the engines, "Mommy's Boy!"

"Shit!" Danny muttered, slightly panicking.

Beside him, a look of incomprehension crossed Jessica's face as she watched the truck come to a halt. Gill, Mitch, her boyfriend Keith, and her friend Mikalya hopped out of the automobile and started heading their way. Annoyed, Jessica ran toward Keith. "What are you doing here? And how the hell did you even find me?" she fired.

However, rather than getting a response, Keith pushed her out of his way, hitting her back against a tree. Danny made an attempt to run to her, but he stopped himself. If he went to them, he would be in the kill zone. He had an advantage as where he stood was an open space. Danny knew he would have to play smart if he was to make it out of Witch's Creek in one piece.

Mikayla had already rushed up to Jessica to check on her and help her up. Danny glanced back, seeing the deeper parts of the forest as he considered making a run for it.

As if reading his thoughts, Keith stated, "You've got nowhere to run, you little bitch."

Danny turned back to face them. There was some truth in the meathead's words, he thought. If he headed into the deeper, uncharted areas of the forest, he could get lost and even find himself in more trouble. Also, he had been running from these bullies for a long time and he was tired of trying to outmaneuver them, hiding away like a chicken. Danny decided it was finally time for him to stand up to them. Besides, he had been going into forests to fetch wood since he was a little boy, and standing where he was, Danny felt like he was in familiar terrain. Even though they were three against him, he believed his chances were good from his vantage point.

Gill and his friends fanned out in an attempt to surround him, with Keith in the vanguard. However, focusing on them more clearly now, Danny noticed something he hadn't at first—a baseball bat was in Gill's hand.

It seemed the same realization had just dawned on Jessica as well. Nursing her arm in pain, she stretched out her hand and cried, "Keith, stop."

Keith ignored her completely. Gill tossed him the bat, and he grabbed it at the handle. He smacked the bat's head against his palm several times; a troubling smirk appeared at the corner of his mouth.

Meanwhile, Mitch had circled around Danny. As he spotted the flower in his hand, he shouted, "Boy, looks like fag stick got your girl a flower."

Danny felt a mixed feeling of thrill and anger. He gripped the flower tightly, squeezing it until he could feel the petals breaking off. Then, he dropped it onto the ground.

Suddenly, a wind began to blow all around them and the trees shook vigorously. As suddenly as it began, it was over in a few seconds, and once again, the forest regained its usual unnerving calmness.

Keith broke the silence. "I need to know the truth, Danny boy. I heard your mom blew everyone in town and once your father found out, he went crazy and killed her," he teased.

Danny's head nearly exploded with rage as he eyed Keith with deadly intent. "Stop!" he warned.

Mitch knew they had the numbers, and he found Danny's threats amusing. He goaded on. "Your psycho pops staged the whole thing and made it look like an accident."

"Fuck you!" Danny retorted. He broke eye contact from all of them, staring at the ground as he watched them in his peripheral vision.

They circled him closer like an eagle hunting its prey. Suddenly, Keith swung the bat at Danny's head. He dodged it and grabbed the bat in midair, staring at Keith dead in the eye. Danny jammed the bat's handle end in Keith's face, hearing the sound of cartilage crunching as his nose bent in an awkward position. Keith moaned in pain as he fell to the ground, grabbing his nose. Blood trickled down from his nostrils.

Danny retrieved the bat and turned to face Mitch. He tossed the bat at him, and Mitch made the costly mistake of grabbing it. His distraction tactic successful, Danny jumped at him with knees flying high. He hit Mitch in the chest, tackling him to the ground. Before Mitch could gather his thoughts, Danny landed three rapid, solid punches in his face. Mitch was defenseless and he tried to scamper away by rolling over. However, Danny flipped him onto his back again and connected his fist with his target's jaw.

"Somebody get him off me!" Mitch cried out.

Meanwhile, Keith was back up on his feet again, his face dripping blood everywhere. He grabbed Danny by the neck in a chokehold but the move had already been anticipated. As his posture left him unbalanced, Danny grabbed his leg and violently pulled, making Keith lose his balance completely and hit his back on the ground hard. He groaned.

Like a ninja, Danny had already rolled up on top of Keith and he began to kick him in the stomach. His feet slammed into the guy's abdominal region relentlessly.

Gill stared at the scene, paralyzed by indecision as he watched his friend cry out for help.

Jessica couldn't take the violence going on around her anymore. "Danny, stop," she pleaded.

Danny was in full rage mode, and he didn't hear a single word of her appeal.

Gill tried to sneak up behind him, but Danny turned around and shot him a warning look; Gill froze in his steps.

With the diversion, Mitch took the opportunity to scamper up and began running toward the truck.

Rather than chase after him, Danny chose to focus on Keith. He grabbed him by the collar and pulled him up, slamming his back against a tree. They stared at each other eye to eye.

"Stopppp, please," Jessica begged again, near tears. Seeing her pleas go unanswered, she attempted to interfere in the heated ongoing fight, but Mikayla held her back, warning her that she could be putting herself in more danger. Jessica remained where she was, silently praying that the fight wouldn't escalate.

Meanwhile, Mitch had climbed up to the back of the pickup truck. He was shuffling around, as if in a desperate search for something. His agitation was visible on his face.

At the battleground, Danny stared at Keith, making the older boy shake in fear. He had beaten them well; now, he wondered what his escape route could be. With such hatred between both parties, he knew they were past the point of resolving their issues through diplomacy. As he pondered, he felt unusual warmth spreading through his arm, which quickly turned to searing pain. Then, he heard a booming noise coming from behind and he staggered, turning to see what it was. He saw Mitch pointing a shotgun at him, with smoke coming out from the round mouth of the gun. Danny glanced down at his shoulder and saw a tear, which had turned into a pooling source of blood, with the viscous liquid flowing freely down his arm onto the muddy ground.

"Danny!" Jessica cried out as she began running toward him. As he fell onto his knees, she got to his side quick enough to catch him in her arms. Jessica wept as she laid him down on the forest floor.

Danny's breath quickened as he began gasping, his head lolling from side to side.

Through his dazed vision, he noticed a shape moving above from one tree to another but he couldn't focus on it.

Meanwhile, Keith was scared shitless as he realized the fight had gone much further than they had antici-pated. All they had planned to do was show the boy some discipline for messing around with his girl; they never thought the little fucker would put up so much resis-tance, and they sure as hell hadn't planned to shoot or kill him. However, Danny was lying on the floor already, losing a lot of blood, and there was nothing any one of them could do to reverse that. "Mitch! Fuck this, man! Fuck!" Keith shouted, panicking.

Jessica cushioned Danny's head in her palm, muttering, "Oh Danny," as she sobbed uncontrollably.

As if Gill had just awoken from a trance, he jolted back to life as he said, "Shit! Shit! Shit!"

Paranoid, Jessica turned her eyes up to the people around. "We need to get him to a hospital!" she pleaded amid tears, her body trembling.

Mitch shook his head in disagreement. "And say what?" he replied, a bone-chilling coldness in his voice.

"He's going to die!" Jessica wailed. She tried to lift him up by herself, but his limp body mass was too much for her strength. He only bulged, semi-conscious. His eyes turned all around as he fell back to the floor.

Thinking on his feet, Keith urged his girlfriend to stop attempting to lift Danny up. An idea had crossed his mind. "No, Jessica. Mitch is right. If we take him to a hospital, they'll ask questions and we'll all end up in jail."

Jessica stared at Keith in disbelief. *How could they just leave him there to die?* she thought. Hysterical, she began to wail, shouting at the top of her voice.

"Bitch, shut the fuck up now!" Mitch yelled at Jessica. Pointing to her and Mikayla, he barked, "Both of you get in the car. Now!" Even without the gun in his hand, he still looked menacing. His hair had mud all over it and his clothes were dirty, his eyeballs bulged like that of a deranged man as he uttered each word.

Gill grabbed the girls by their arms. Jessica tried to wriggle off but he tightened his grip, his long nails digging into her skin as he dragged both girls like rag dolls toward the pickup truck. "Come on!" he barked.

The sun was beginning to go down already and the sunlight was starting to dim. Gill tossed the girls into the car. "Let me go, you son of a bitch," Jessica yelled hysterically, slapping Gill rapidly in the face a few times.

The slaps stung, but Gill didn't retaliate; he had enough on his plate already. "Stay put, girls, or else…" He left the threat hanging as he locked the car doors and went back to join friends.

As quickly as he had left, Jessica and Mikayla quickly turned around to watch the scene from the back window.

"We need to bury him," Keith suggested, arms akimbo. Mitch seemed unconvinced. "Bury him with what?" he asked.

Mitch was stumped. He hadn't thought it through. "Shit! Shit!" he muttered furiously, with saliva flying out of his mouth as he did.

Danny tried to stand up again, staggering. The boys around watched him but none of them made a move to help him up. Danny almost made it to his feet alone but his legs buckled and faltered; he stumbled onto the cold, forest ground once more with a thud.

As Mitch watched him crumble to the ground, a cynical idea struck him. "The wolves. The wolves will finish him off... There won't be any evidence. We're at least ten miles from town. No one comes here, not even hunters; there are too many wolves," he rambled.

The idea didn't sit well with Keith. Images of what the scene would look like flowed through his mind, and he began to panic. He couldn't go with the wolf carnage plan; instead, he concluded that they needed to improvise. "Gill, check if there's anything useful in the truck," he ordered.

Gill jogged over to the truck in search of what they could use for damage control.

Meanwhile, Danny had flipped onto his belly and began to crawl in the opposite direction, where the forest was thicker. However, he could only move at a snail's pace as his strength was nearly depleted. Intrigued, Mitch crouched beside him, watching him with amusement. "You pathetic, little shit," he said, slapping Danny at the back of his head, making him groan and cough out blood.

Then, Gill hurried back with a long roll of barbwire in his hands. "What will we do with fucking barbwire?" Keith demanded, puzzled. "It'll do nicely," Mitch replied, smirking mischievously.

Gill twirled the barbwire in his hand. A jagged end of the wire cut his finger. "Ow!" he remarked, sucking the finger.

"Gill, grab Danny," Keith suggested. With mouth ajar, Gill asked, "Why me?"

"Come on, pussy, we're losing time," Mitch said.

The two of them knelt down. Mitch picked up Danny's arms, and Gill grabbed his feet.

Together, they began heaving him to a nearby tree. They'd hardly arrived when Danny's shoulders cracked and dislocated. Scared, Gill quickly dropped him and jumped back. Undeterred, Mitch grabbed the body roughly and plopped it against the bark of the tree.

In the truck, Jessica couldn't watch anymore and she turned her head down, sobbing into the chair. Mikayla looked restless on her own but still, she placed her arm across her friend's shoulder, comforting her. "Shh... It's okay, no one will find out," she whispered soothingly.

Jessica looked into her eyes as if she had gone mad. How could she be friends with someone that was okay with murder? She shoved Mikayla away.

By then, it was getting so late that only a little glint of light reached the forest grounds as many of the trees had blocked most of the sun rays. Keith handed the barbwire to Gill; he, in turn, passed it to Mitch.

Unrolling some length off the bundle of the jagged ended metal wire, Mitch walked around the tree. He then kicked in a piece of the barbwire firmly into the bark of the tree. "You guys might wanna close your eyes," he warned.

Taking the priceless warning, Gill and Keith instantly turned their backs to what was about to happen. Keith shut his eyes tightly, grimacing as he heard building muffled moans coming from behind him; he didn't want to know what was going on.

Danny began screaming in deep pain, startling Jessica, who sat in the truck. She hid her head in between the chair and placed her hands over her ears. She prayed for it all to end.

Mitch had twisted the barbwire around Danny, tying him to the tree. He dusted his blood-covered hands off on his pants as he stood back and observed his handiwork. He clicked his tongue as he stared at the barbwire. There was still some space between the wires and Danny's chest as he was still able to move. Mitch couldn't accept that. "Guys, we need to make it tighter," he called out.

Keith glanced back and was terrified by the sight before him. "I'm not touching that thing," he stated, shaking his head vigorously.

Gill, on the other hand, wasn't too mushy about it. He looked all around before suggesting, "We could use the truck."

"Hurry! Go now," Mitch ordered.

Gill ran to the truck and hopped into the driver's seat. Turning the ignition, he put the gear in reverse and revved. Mitch was holding one end of the barbwire; he walked up to the truck and tied it to the bumper.

He signaled to Gill to hit the gas pedal. The car began moving slowly.

The coiled barbwire began to straighten and it started tightening around Danny. The wires dug into his skin, ripping his flesh like paper.

Danny cried out.

Mitch seemed to be enjoying the sadistic act as he smiled and signaled Gill to keep on moving the truck.

Keith was unsettled by this. "Alright… Alright… I think that's enough. Gill! Stop the fucking truck!" he barked.

Gill revved one last time, sending blood flying around, a slop landing on Mitch's face, before he stopped the truck.

Keith quickly ran to the pickup and untied the barbwire from the bumper. "Let's get the fuck outta here." He climbed to the back of the truck and dropped the barbwire there. Everyone was in the truck and ready to leave, all except for Mitch.

"What the hell are you still waiting for, man?" Gill called out to him but got no response.

Mitch was still preoccupied with Danny. He kicked the rest of the barbwire into the tree bark and knelt beside Danny, whose head drooped. He placed his hand beneath his chin, raising his head up. "You know no one's going to miss you," he whispered into Danny's ear.

"Let's go now!" Keith shouted from the back of the truck, but Mitch ignored him; he wasn't done yet. He dipped his hand inside his pocket and pulled out a switchblade. Danny's eyes widened. Slowly, Mitch buried the knife below Danny's ribs while grinning heartily. Just as slowly as the knife went in, Mitch pulled it out, slightly twisting it.

Danny was already numb with pain, and he couldn't feel much of the effect of this last assault on him; only his organs did.

Mitch patted his cheeks twice before standing up. As he prepared to leave, he took one last glance at Danny. "See ya around," he said.

He strutted to the pickup to join his friends. Soon enough, the truck began to back out toward the main road. Its occupants tried to keep their cool, with the exception of Keith, who was slowly losing his mouth. "We fucked up, man. We fucked up big time," he said repeatedly, smacking his palm against his face. Gill yelled at him to shut his mouth and get his shit together. Still, this proved ineffective in calming him.

As the truck began to leave, Jessica stared out of the back window, her eyes glued on Danny, whose head rocked back and forth as he fought to stay conscious.

Danny kept his eyes on the truck, watching it disappear into the distance. As it rounded a corner and went completely out of sight, his hope totally depleted. Danny let out a final blood-chilling roar and then bowed his head in resignation; he succumbed to his fate and waited impatiently for the grim reaper.

In his final moments, Danny had a divine experience: He saw his mother, beautiful, much younger than he remembered. She was looking down into a crib and smiling at a six- month-old baby. In an eye-widening revelation, Danny realized the baby was him. However, he was too young then to be able to recollect so much. Besides, he was watching the scene as a bystander, not from the baby's eyes. It felt like he just had a first-hand experience of astral projection and time travel; the sensation was overwhelming but equally soothing. As his brain worked overtime trying to make sense of what he was seeing, everything went black.

Once again, a wind began to blow through the forest; this time, it was more intense. It shook the trees at their roots, and the branches bent sideways. Like the sound of a gigantic cricket chirping, a noise began to come from the denser parts of the forest. A branch snapped overhead but fell to the ground except for leaves of various kinds.

By then, Danny was beyond frightened as he had nearly lost all sensation. However, he could feel the presence of an entity approaching him from the depths of the forest. With his blurry vision, all he could make out was the shape of a humanoid figure. Danny tried to pull himself free, but the barbwire was still wound tight around. As if in a way of cautioning him to stay put, the wire began to rip into his flesh again, cutting into his biceps. Danny cursed under his breath as he gritted his teeth. He let out an audible sigh as began to relax, waiting for the person approaching him to grant him a mercy-killing.

Regardless of what he did, he was inches away from death anyway, he admitted.

The tree he rested his back against began to shake. Above, small twigs began to drop, catching Danny's attention. With unfocused eyes, he looked up and the sight he saw nearly made his weakened heart stop for good. Danny saw a girl's body hanging from the tree. Even though he couldn't make out her face in the darkness, the position of her body and the dress she had on made Danny come to a chilling realization—it was her, the one from the story who was burnt and hanged in this same forest for being a witch. It was Ida.

As if on cue, a dark figure began to crawl down the tree. Danny couldn't tell what the body of the sinister entity looked like. From where he sat, all he could see was a grotesque burnt hand slowly working its way down the thick tree.

Danny's head kept on drooping and he struggled to keep it up. From behind the tree, a hand touched his face, gently massaging his wounds. Danny had anticipated a cold, callous sensation, however, the hand was very soft and the touch soothing; he began to weaken to the sensation.

Slowly, Ida walked around from the back of the tree, never taking her eyes off Danny's as she finally stood before him. Even though his sight wasn't clear, Danny could still see that she was truly beautiful, with her long, flowing, golden hair, vibrant blue eyes, and a seductive, voluptuous body.

He tried to keep his gaze but his strength failed him. As his head dropped to his chest once again, Ida knelt before him and lifted it back up. "Pain… Suffering," she said in a coarse, wispy voice.

As she spoke, the sounds of a hundred paws and hooves began to echo all around. At first, Danny couldn't see anything past the darkness. As he tried to focus, he saw several little animals on the forest floor scampering toward him. Huge spiders, he thought at first.

However, as they got closer, he noticed the animals were furrier than the arachnids. They were hopping quickly. Rabbits? Squirrels? Finally, he saw their tails as they gathered around—they were indeed squirrels. Instantly, other shapes began to appear from behind trees, all of them staring at Danny. From their long antlers, he could tell that it was a group of deer.

At that moment, a howl pierced the air, which was instantly answered by several others. From all directions, black wolves began to emerge. They began to walk toward the tree where Danny was tied. He was going to be eaten by wolves and finally relieved of his pain and suffering, he thought. He made no attempt to move as he knew it was a futile effort that could only result in more pain.

All the animals of various species, both predators and prey, formed an unusual alliance under the power of a supernatural force as they converged behind Ida to form a semi-circle around the tree. Ida glanced back, admiring the effect of her conjuring. She turned her attention back to Danny. She looked at him intently, solely focusing on his left eye, and then his right, as if she was staring at a conduit that provided direct access to his soul. In her raspy voice, she began saying, "Evil hearts want us dead... Become the darkness you have in your heart. Avenge us, my prince..."

She rubbed the back of her palm against Danny's cheek affectionately. With the touch, all his defenses went down; his soul was bare. "I can't..." he whispered, his weakness apparent in his voice.

Ida placed a finger on Danny's lips. "Don't speak," she cautioned. "Darken your heart... Use your pain."

As she uttered the words, her skin began to crisp into a burnt-looking corpse, and her beautiful dress turned into a dirty, lice-infested robe of rags. Danny's eyes widened in incomprehension but before he could register what was happening, the witch snapped the barbwire like twigs and then shoved her hands into the wounds in his torso. He tried to protest but his voice seized in his throat.

Dark roots began to sprout from the muddy ground around the tree Danny rested against. Slowly, the roots began to intertwine as they wrapped around him. There was no escape. All Danny could do was look up to the sky, momentarily noticing how there were no stars to grace the world's roof that night. Memories began to fill his head, both old and recent ones, appearing like a massive photo collage. He saw the scene of Ida's hanging, how the townspeople had stood around watching until the life went out of her and the fire consumed her to chars. The images drifted to that of his dad, in the good old days when Danny was a young boy and his pops hadn't started drinking. The memory was of when David first took his son hunting, showing him how to bag a prize from afar. As quickly as the memory appeared in his head, it dissolved to that of his mother, patting his head as he cried in her lap over skinned knees. Finally, Jessica came into focus, the way he knew her at that point in time. She smiled at him, her eyes complementing her beauty; there was nothing retro about her smile. He had to take the chance with the witch if he was to see Jessica again. He let his guard down completely and yielded to the witch's probing.

Danny's eyes turned glassy black as a supernatural spirit descended upon him. He let out a roar, which was instantly picked up by the wolves as they howled beneath the night sky. The resulting cacophony was more than enough to frighten anyone a few miles away.

3

HOME

Mikayla yelped as the truck rocked.

"Relax, it's just a bump," Gill said, in an attempt to calm her; it didn't work as her eyes still roamed about wildly as if something was going to jump at them from out of the woods.

Suddenly, the noise of wolf howls pierced the air. On hearing it, Mitch smirked, feeling elated as he imagined that the howls were a gratuitous call for the dinner he had left for them.

Gill, however, heard an ungodly bellow that carried much louder than the wolf cries. "What monster lay in this forest at night?" he uttered rhetorically. He didn't want to find out the answer. Gill stepped his foot on the accelerator, ignoring the protests for caution from the other occupants of the vehicle. However, he didn't ease the pressure on the pedal until they had passed the Witch's Creek welcoming signpost.

"We're out of the woods now," he said, sighing in relief. Gill began to whistle as he began cooking up a cover-up story in his head. At that moment, the most important thing was that he and his friends were safe, he thought.

Officer Teresa flipped through the pages of the report on her desk. The town was a relatively safe one, and the biggest crimes the authorities had had to handle recently were hooliganism-related. Not that she was looking for some action—she enjoyed the free time she got to take off work to engage in miscellaneous activities. At that, the thought of Danny crossed her mind; how he had ravaged her body in the laundry room at their last encounter. Her body tingled, making her smile as she anticipated seeing Danny again soon.

Her office door creaked open and a male colleague stepped in. "Hi, gorgeous," Officer Doug said, smiling like a little boy who had just discovered the hidden pleasure in licorice after a first taste. Doug sported a short, dyed-blond haircut. Although he was in his early thirties, his oval face and its soft features gave him the appearance of a teenager. As such, he looked charming in a non-threatening way, and Teresa found him more amusing than sexually appealing.

"How can I help you?" she asked without taking her eyes off the papers in front of her.

Doug's bright demeanor quickly turned down a few notches. He hadn't expected her to regard him curtly. This made his expression change to that of a hurt puppy. In an attempt to warm her up a bit, he replied, "I can think of a thing or two."

Teresa glanced at him, staring him in the eyes. After a long and pregnant beat of silence, Doug realized she wasn't in the mood for any jokes. "I'm only kidding," he chuckled nervously, his attempt to break the ice failing.

He tossed the file he held onto Teresa's desk. "We had multiple people call in a three- eleven, all around Witch's Creek." He paused, trying to remember the other detail in the report. He quickly ruffled through the papers before adding, "And... Yes, someone heard a gun go off."

Teresa shrugged. "Probably a hunter."

"I doubt that. No one hunts in Witch's Creek anymore."

Unconvinced, Teresa grabbed the files from the desk and began reading. After going through a few pages, she came across something that made her stop reading. She looked up at Doug and cocked her eyebrow. "A roar?" she asked, referencing what she saw in the file.

Doug nodded. Stars danced in his eyes, and it was glaringly obvious that he was excited by the enthusiasm showed by his colleague.

Without wasting a single second longer, Teresa grabbed her jacket off the arm of her chair. Setting her hat on her head as she stood up, she ordered, "Let's go."

The full moon shone brightly that night. However, the dense forest of Witch's Creek didn't allow it passage to oversee what was going on in the undergrowth. Only a little glint of light pierced through the resistant vegetation. This sparse light was enough for Danny to navigate through the woods as his black eyes seemed accustomed to the darkness. Danny's legs wobbled, and he leaned on trees from one to the other for support as he stumbled through the forest. Danny noticed the trees beginning to shift and sway with every breath he took, seemingly connected to the forest.

The farther he got, the more strength he gained. Soon enough, he was out of the woods, his posture slouched as he began stomping toward home in the darkness.

For minutes on end, he walked. By the time he got to the mobile home, it was very late in the night and he didn't come across a single soul.

Danny stomped up the porch. Suddenly, out of the darkness, Zeus jumped at him, growling. Danny retreated a few paces.

Recognizing and sensing his owner, the Doberman stopped barking and walked closer to snuggle Danny's legs. He rubbed his dog's head affectionately, wondering how long Zeus had been standing outside waiting for him. He approached the door, his loyal companion closely behind him.

He searched his pocket for keys; he couldn't find them. After the entire scuffle that had gone down in the forest, he wasn't surprised he had lost them.

He couldn't waste any more time waiting around; Danny reached out his hand and grabbed the doorknob, hoping it was unlocked. However, as he twisted the metal knob, it snapped, leaving an imprint. Danny was surprised by the inhuman strength he now possessed. He needed answers.

He tossed the broken doorknob aside. Once he and Zeus were inside, he slammed the door behind them and hurried to his room. Inside, he pulled off his torn cloth that had already been caked with mud and blood. Danny stood in front of the mirror and ran his eyes all over his body. Covering him from the side of his head down to his waist were dried, dirty blood marks. His eyes lingered on his wounds, the prominent ones being the small hole in his shoulder made by the bullet, the gash beneath his ribs where he had been stabbed, and the deep cuts carved into his chest by the barbwire. The witch's touch had sealed up the wounds; however, Danny could see bulging, dark veins running like cable wires under the flesh around his injuries. He couldn't look anymore.

Danny turned around. Dragging his feet, he began walking down the hall. Zeus followed him, licking his legs in concern. However, the Doberman soon met some resistance in the form of a bathroom door, which his master shut quietly in his face.

Danny slipped out of his pants and stood under the shower. He slowly turned the control knob all the way to the right, doing it carefully so as not to break that too. The outlet made a hissing noise as steaming water began to stream out. Danny placed his head directly under the water, pretending the warm liquid was washing away his tribulations.

In the hallway, Zeus sat quietly by the bathroom door. Suddenly he jumped up and began barking as he heard sinister growls and roars coming from where his master had just entered to take his bath. Zeus began scratching at the door, looking for ways to bring down the barrier so he could go defend his master from the monster who roared ferociously.

Little did the loyal Doberman know that his master was the monster.

4

INCHES

Ding ding! The school bell echoed across the premises.

Gillian walked down the hall, his eyes darting around nervously. When he spotted Keith, he beckoned him with a nod, and together they began heading toward the class. No single word was exchanged between the duo until they stepped through the classroom door.

Inside, Gill stood in front of the class, his eyes canvassing the faces of the occupants of the room. Many of them stared right back at him with quizzical looks on their faces. He sighed audibly with relief as he noticed that both Jessica and Danny were absent. With nervous steps, he went to take his seat.

The bell rang again.

As if on cue, Mrs. Hork click-clacked into the class

and headed directly for the board. "Good morning, class." Turning around, she took in the environment. Her eyes narrowed as she said, "It appears two students didn't make it to class today...." She paused, and then called out, "Gillian!"

Gill's eyes widened, and his head popped up. "Yes... Yes, ma'am," he stuttered, nearly falling out of his seat as he heard his name being called unexpectedly.

"Do you have any idea why they are absent?" the teacher asked.

Gill shook his head quickly in denial. "Uhhh... No, not at all," he blurted out. Instantly, he averted his gaze as if the woman could read the lies by looking into his eyes.

"Hmm. Okay then." Mrs. Hork didn't catch the signs from his uneasiness. Addressing the whole class, she said, "Please pull out your notes from last week and turn to page sixty- six."

For the second time that day, Gill let out a long-drawn sigh. He slowly placed his head on his desk, saying silent prayers, words of which that hadn't passed through his mouth in over a decade ago. As the moment passed, he jolted back into an upright position and faced the teacher. He jotted some notes down briefly before placing his pen in the book, bookmarking the page where he had stopped. He was getting bored of the class already.

Suddenly, the classroom door squeaked open slowly, inch after inch. All eyes in the room turned to the door, expecting to see who the sneaky latecomer was. However, several seconds passed and the only thing that entered the room was a gentle breeze. Seeing that there was no intruder, Mrs. Hork walked over to close the door that stood ajar.

"Hmm. A little breeze is all we have here." The teacher turned to face the class. In a light-hearted voice, she said, "Now, where were we?"

As she began to walk to the board, the door opened again, this time with a louder creak.

Startled, Mrs. Hork quickly turned around. "Hello? Who's there?" She stuck her head into the hallway and instantly retracted it as an overwhelmed expression crossed her face. "Danny? What in heaven's name happened to you? Oh my god!"

Gill's eyes nearly popped out of his head in shock as his vision began to spin. He gripped the arm of his chair tightly. "What the hell," he muttered.

Suddenly a force pushed his chair, making Gill lean forward. He quickly glanced behind; none of the students were standing up, and the nearest chair to him was still several inches away.

Fear was starting to weave a deep nest in his heart. Just then, his desk began to jolt noisily as if being kicked. Gill held the chair's arm tighter, nearly jumping up. More baffling was the fact that there was no visible person kicking the desk. However, it jolted again and again.

Gill's erratic behavior was drawing the attention of his classmates. Dreading what was to come, he considered making a run for it. As he tried to spring up, something grabbed him by the neck. His heart nearly failed him as he saw Danny standing directly over him. His eyes were completely black as if his irises had been coated with a hue of darkness. Under his eyes, where sleep bags usually were lodged, were dark, thick veins. Thinking he was seeing a ghost of some sort, Gill became petrified.

"I'm not dead," Danny said in an eerie metallic voice as he branded a sharp-edged ruler in his spare hand and sliced Gill's throat with it in one swift motion, the unmistakable sound of gargling serving as a soundtrack for the gory scene.

With eyes closed, Gill screamed out and landed on the floor. Surprisingly, rather than shrieking in horror, all he heard from the people around him was laughter. He quickly scampered up and opened his eyes to see his classmates pointing and laughing at him. With great relief, he realized he had seen Danny in a dream, a very bad one.

Beads of sweat rolled off his face, some dropping in his eyes, stinging him. His vision became dizzy. Still feeling restless with guilt, Gill began to run, pushing Mrs. Hork out of the way without a word of apology as he stormed out of the class.

"Gillian!" the teacher shouted after him, but he was gone. Mrs. Hork looked troubled as she was bothered by his unusual paranoia. She made a mental note to call him to her office the next morning.

Meanwhile, Gill was dashing down the hallway at near superhuman speed. He rushed into the boy's bathroom heading straight to the faucet and turned on the tap. He scooped some water and poured it on his face. He began to breathe heavily as he stared at himself in the mirror.

Gill caught a shadow out of the corner of his eye. Instantly, he whirled around and was both grateful and disappointed to see nobody. Parts of his brain needed a logical explanation for all the bizarre things he had been experiencing all day. Again, he let out a heavy breath in an attempt to calm himself; it didn't work.

Suddenly, a toilet seat plopped down, making a loud noise. Gill nearly jumped out of his skin. "Hey, who's there?" he called out.

His voice bounced around the walls of the small restroom. However, nobody responded.

Gill began to approach the cubicle where the noise had originated, walking nearly on tiptoe, moving stealthily as much as his bulky frame would allow. As he got closer, he looked beneath the stalls but there were no legs visible. As he got to the last stall, his heart began to pound faster, afraid and relieved for what he may find.

Just before he peered through the stall door, Gill was interrupted by a student who made his way toward the urinal. Gill immediately retreated toward the sink, eyeing down the student in the urinal through the mirror. Trying to regain his nerve, he turned his attention toward the sink, turning on the faucet.

The faucet began to shutter as if clogged, the clear inconsistent flow of water began to turn a muddy black, grabbing Gill's attention. The student on the other side of the bathroom began to silently twitch in the distance as his head slowly cracked, making a full one-eighty-degree turn toward Gill. The student slowly walked toward Gill, stopping directly behind him.

Oblivious to what was happening around him, Gill turned off the faucet, feeling a chill on the back of his neck. Looking back into the reflection, he realized the student was gone. Gill quickly turned to an empty stall, as rising confusion and paranoia built within him.

Gill began running toward the exit. Outside, he stopped to catch his breath. Panting heavily to steady his feeble heart, he leaned forward and placed his palms on his thighs. He glanced left and right, feeling utterly alone. As he made to leave, he noticed a shadow on the reflective tiled floor, seeming to grow and approach him from behind. However, his brain registered the danger a second too late.

As Gill's thick legs were instantly pulled with great force, Gill's head slammed hard into the cold floor, his jaw making a cracking noise like he was chewing a mouthful of chips. He passed out instantly. Gill's plopped body began being dragged back into the bathroom. His cheek smeared blood onto the floor as a chipped tooth came out of his mouth, leaving a bloody souvenir just by the open entrance.

⁓

Keith stared at the board absentmindedly; the equations written on it looked like doodles to him. His head was preoccupied with the erratic behavior Gill had displayed earlier. When his friend had stormed out of the class like a deranged man, he had wanted to go after him but he chose not to. He didn't want to raise any suspicions. However, he still wondered what had made him run off like that. As he pondered the possibilities, his phone buzzed in his pocket.

Keith quickly pulled it out and glanced at it. "Speak of the devil," he muttered.

Displayed on the smartphone's screen was a text from Gill, which read, *Bathroom, come quick.*

Keith stared at the screen for a few seconds longer. "What the fuck," he whispered to himself. There was only one way to find out. Keith closed the book in front of him and dashed out of the class without asking for permission.

His sneakers glossed over the smoothly tiled floors of the hallway. It was empty at that time of the day, except for two freshmen he passed by. Soon enough, he skidded to a stop right outside the entrance of the bathroom. He dashed inside without hesitation and nearly slipped as he stepped on the smeared, red liquid on the floor. Keith realized it was blood, and lying in the trek of it was a small, ceramic-like object. Even before he picked it up, Keith could tell what it was—a once-sparkling, white tooth which had now been tainted with crimson red. Danger lurked around, he quickly cautioned himself. He decided to flee to get some help as he didn't know what he would face.

Just then, "Keeeeiiitth…" he heard someone call out in a weak voice. Keith was nearly out the bathroom entrance, but at the sound of his name, he quickly stopped running and stood still as his eyes darted around. "Gill… Gill is that you?" he replied with a loud whisper.

"Keittth!" the voice called out again a little louder. From the tone, it was deducible that the person was in deep pain.

Keith knew he had to act. He looked down at the bloodstain on the floor. Gingerly stepping around it to avoid getting the incriminating evidence on his shoes, he began to follow the blood trail from its unfortunate source.

"Gill!" he said as he got closer. No response; all he could hear was a low groan. He stopped in front of the middle stall. "I can see your shoes, idiot," he called out. Keith hesitated for a second, dreading what he would find inside. However, he knew his friend had likely been harmed and if he was, he needed to help him. "Damn it," he lamented.

Summoning all his courage, he let out a long sigh

before kicking in the door. Instantly, he regretted his decision to barge in. The sight before him was incomprehensible. Keith jumped back, slipping on a small puddle of blood, landing his ass on the floor at the sight he beheld; sitting in his friend's blood had become inconsequential.

Gill lay sprawled on the toilet seat, and the blood was only coming from one region of his body—his face. Perfectly lodged in his right eye was a thick, wooden ruler. Nothing of the previous occupant of the space could be seen as the ruler had taken sole tenancy of his right eye socket.

He was stunned for a moment. However, a noise from the next stall jolted him back to his precarious position. From his point of view, he could see a dirty pair of loafers beneath the stall. The door wasn't closed properly, and Keith slowly began moving his eye up, staring through the crack. His heart pounded loudly as he made eye contact with the stall's sole occupant—Danny.

Danny stared at him with inviting, black eyes and a smirk.

"No fucking way! Fuck! *Fuck!*" Keith began shouting as he crawled up and ran out of the restroom frantically.

"Keith… Keith!" Gill shouted after him in a sinister yet familiar voice. Just then, his voice began to gain some depth as he began laughing, his cackles ringing inside Keith's head as he ran down the hall, his heels on fire. A disturbing memory permanently seared in his brain.

———

Jessica lay on her queen-sized bed, a fluffy pillow crumpled beneath her head. The room was beautifully designed and furnished, a reflection of the elegance that dominated in other parts of the house. The big, Victorian-style building her father had erected a couple of decades ago still stood strong. The commuters of the road that passed in front of the house often took their eyes off the road to steal glances at the aesthetically pleasing edifice. Jessica often thought that if it had been a major road that many vehicles ferried, several accidents would've occurred as a result of the distraction her home posed.

Jessica turned in her bed, burying her face in the pillow. The day was warm, giving the room a comfortable glow. However, none of the comforts in her home could soothe the ache in her heart. Her shoulders shook as she sobbed uncontrollably, muffling her cries with the pillow.

Each time memories of Danny came to her mind, waves of sorrow washed over her. Whenever she remembered his sweet goofiness, the images were quickly replaced with the gory ones of the scene of his death.

Jessica blamed herself for standing idly by when the fight in Witch's Creek began to take a dark turn. She should've done something when the boys began to tie Danny to the tree like an animal. She kept wondering how much pain and suffering he must have endured alone in that sinister forest. Jessica became more uneasy as she recalled the howls they had heard when they escaped the forest. Maybe the wolves had found Danny and were giving a joyful cheer before they tore into their unexpected dinner.

Suddenly, Jessica's phone began to ring. She jolted upright, irritated by the noise that interrupted her mourning. She leaned over to pick up her phone from the nightstand. The device still belted out a slow, melodious ringtone, and the accompanying caller ID indicated it was Keith calling. Jessica hissed in annoyance and silenced the call. He was the last person in the universe she wanted to speak to.

As the call ended without going to voicemail, Jessica stepped into a pair of flip-flops and started out her bedroom door. She decided she couldn't allow herself to break down by wallowing in bed all day so she climbed down the stairs and headed for the kitchen, which was conveniently located just adjacent to the living room. She walked up to the cupboard and got out a box of cereal. Setting a small, ceramic bowl on the kitchen counter, she shook some of the cereal into the bowl. Noticing the television remote on the counter, she picked it up and turned on the TV. Before it could come on, Jessica had turned her back already to get some milk.

A local news channel came up on the television, a slightly-balding male reporter was saying, "…the authorities are still underway investigating the disturbing murder at J Tower School…"

They had found him, Jessica thought. Like a boot-strapped sailor thrown into an ocean, her heart sank. She rummaged through the shelves angrily for the milk, her back still turned to the television. Her eyes became teary, and she banged her fist against a cupboard door.

In a voice trained to dispense bad news with as much cushion as possible, the reporter continued, "…Gilbert Thomas was found dead earlier this morning…"

Instantly, Jessica cocked her ears and glanced at the

television. What the hell was the man talking about?

The scene on the screen was shot in front of her school, and she was undoubtedly sure that the Gilbert Thomas mentioned was none other than Gill. She was sure she heard the reporter say murder, not suicide. *Who would've wanted to kill Gill?* she thought.

"…Investigators will have more information later tonight…"

She needed to know what the hell was going on. Jessica picked up her phone and saw a few missed calls and text notifications from both Keith and Mikayla. She quickly opened the first text from Keith, which read, *He's alive, meet us at Frank Park by one pm.*

Jessica's neurons began firing on overload as a million questions popped up in her head within seconds. Who murdered Gill? What was so big that Keith couldn't say over the phone and wanted to meet her in person? Was it to confess that he had killed Gill? What did he mean by, 'he's alive?' Was he referring to Danny or Gill? These lines of questions went on and on in her head and she began to feel overwhelmed. Jessica knew she couldn't get the answers she wanted by staying where she was. She had to go see Keith.

She checked her phone again for a message from

Mikayla. *What's going on? I'm so scared*, it read. Jessica quickly typed a response, *Meet up at Frank Park... Be there by one*.

With that, Jessica hurried upstairs to get dressed.

5

I SEE YOU

Keith paced nervously around the center of the huge field where he and Mitch stood. "How's it possible?" he asked.

"Relax, Keith," Mitch replied in a hushed tone.

"Don't tell me to relax, man! You don't get to do that shit anymore, telling me what to do!"

Mitch stretched out his arms, his palms facing forward as he gestured for peace.

"Okay, cool it, man." This seemed to have the opposite effect on his friend as he began to pace around more quickly. Mitch continued, "The only explanation for this shitstorm is that the little bastard must have slipped off the barbwire and probably walked home."

Keith looked unconvinced. "If that crazy scenario had happened, why didn't he go to the hospital? You shot him, Mitch, and he was gushing blood. He—he fucking killed Gill."

Mitch shook his head in anger. "Those weirdoes are really crazy. We should've put the boy down a long time ago."

Keith stared at him incredulously. "Or maybe you shouldn't have tried to kill him at all. Now, that shit has come back to bite us in the nuts."

As the boys continued to argue about their mistakes, Jessica and Mikayla began to approach from the distance.

When the girls got close enough, the group of four huddled together. None of them said any greetings. The tension between them was high.

"Why did you call me here?" Jessica stated blatantly in a cold voice. She addressed the question to her boyfriend, or unofficial ex-boyfriend. She stared him in the eye, ignoring his murderous friend completely as if he didn't exist.

Keith's eyes reflexively roamed around the premise, as if scared of someone overhearing their conversation even though they were alone in the middle of the field and there was nobody else anywhere near them. Then he said, "Your little lover is alive."

"You mean Danny's alive?" Jessica asked, looking incredulous as stars danced around her eyes.

"Yeah, yeah. Don't sound too excited," Keith replied, feeling a slight pang of jealousy in the pit of his stomach.

"Fuck you," Jessica yelled furiously. Suddenly, she stretched out her hand and landed a resounding slap on Keith's cheek. His hand quickly went up to his reddened face, his ears ringing painfully. Infuriated, he slapped her back and pushed her with force.

Jessica lost her footing and fell onto the dusty ground. "You fucking pig…" she shouted in annoyance. Mikayla quickly rushed to her side and helped her up. Jessica brushed the dirt off her clothes. Noticing her bruised elbow, her face reddened in anger. She looked up at Keith with a death stare; he glared back at her with matching rage in his eyes.

Meanwhile, a few yards away behind them were a pair of black eyes well-hidden behind the cover of trees, watching the scene in the park. Danny tapped his foot nervously as he watched Keith push Jessica. He wanted to rush out and rip off his head, but he cautioned himself. "Patience, patience," he said under his breath. His ultra-focused eyes roved all over the area, canvassing the field and seeing them clearly as if he was standing among them.

Mitch shifted with unease. "Look, guys, we need a really good plan."

"We should go to the cops," Mikayla suggested. She was scared out of her mind due to the precarious situation they had found themselves in, but she was wary of the people she was standing with as she had seen how dangerous they could get.

"Bitch, I said a good plan," Mitch retorted.

Keith looked unsure, contemplating the best way to resolve their deadly issue. Things were getting out of hand pretty fast. They were at a huge disadvantage as they can't tell others what they had done and why Danny was coming after them. The last time he had encountered him, Danny looked like a monster from the scariest of nightmares. Keith wondered if they had truly killed him and his ghost was now haunting them. Shit has gone awry enough; Gill was dead, he thought. They needed to act fast or else they could be next, he concluded. He started saying their options out loud. "If we go to the cops, we are all toast. If we…"

"We need to finish him off," Mitch interjected.

Instantly, all eyes turned to him. Keith wondered if his friend wasn't actually a real psychopath all along.

"Nah, I'm out. Mikayla and I are done, we had no part in all this mess," Jessica stated. She glanced at her friend who looked as confused and scared as a chicken dropped to fly from an airplane. Jessica nudged her head toward the exit, beckoning her. Together, they began to leave.

"Don't you dare walk away from me," Keith called out.

Jessica glanced back briefly, throwing him a middle finger as she turned her head back and started walking out of the park.

"Come back here!" Keith shouted in a coarse voice. Getting no response, he gritted his teeth and threw his fist in the air, exasperated.

Just then, a gentle breeze began to blow in the forest around, making the trees swerve back and forth. Mitch's eyes darted around, paranoid as the hair on his arms stood up. He stared deeper into the woods, sensing that an entity was close by, watching him. After a few seconds of scrutinizing the forest with his eyes and seeing nothing out of the ordinary, he shook off the feeling of uneasiness. Maybe he was indeed finally losing his mind. From beside him, he heard Keith say, "We need to keep an eye on these girls. No loose ends."

"Yes. Yes, we should," Mitch responded, nodding absentmindedly.

The silence was profound as the two girls walked down the footpath in the woods. The only sound other than that of their feet crunching on dead leaves was a low whooshing noise that dominated the air.

Mikayla and Jessica walked side by side, each one oblivious that at that moment different thoughts on the same topic were going through their heads. Mikayla was the first to speak. "I heard that some people don't stay dead after they've been killed. Do you think he's..."

"It's not our fault. I tried to stop him," Jessica replied. She cocked her head slightly, seeming lost in thoughts. Finally, she said, "I keep wondering how they knew Danny and I were in Witch's Creek."

Instantly, Mikayla went mute. She stared straight ahead, her body slightly trembling as a result of discomfort.

Jessica's eyes grew thin, and she stopped walking, eyeing her friend as she fidgeted nervously, which was unusual of her. Jessica became skeptical. "Mikayla," she called out.

As if anticipating the question, Mikayla raised her head higher, shrinking her neck; she stopped dead in her tracks and turned around slowly.

Jessica stared at her in the eye, trying to read her expression. "Mikayla," she repeated in a softer and more threatening tone.

Mikayla lost her composure and busted into tears. "Mitch begged me! He told me he loved me…"

"You told him," Jessica stated, her eyes growing thinner with each word until her eyelids were so close she couldn't see anything beyond a squint.

Mikayla began sobbing. "Pleassseee…." she begged amid tears.

Jessica shook her head in disbelief and took a step forward.

Seeing her advancing, Mikayla quickly gathered herself and shuffled a few paces backward.

Jessica chuckled at her cowardice. She was deeply pained by her friend's betrayal which may have cost Danny his life or at the very least—if she chose to believe the words of Keith, that he had become a sadistic killer—his sanity. "This is your fault," she said, her voice carrying her pain and anguish.

Mikayla stared at the ground, afraid to provoke Jessica even more if she maintained eye contact with her. She cowered where she stood, attempting to move her feet but she couldn't. The overwhelming shame had rooted her to the spot.

Jessica walked up to her and stood beside her. With their backs to each other, she glanced sideways and saw the petrified look on her face. She felt neither pity nor compassion for her pathetic act. "I hope the dick was worth it," she said, feeling a slight enjoyment watching her cower in fear. "Walk yourself home, bitch," she added. With that, she started walking away.

Mikayla turned around, her heart thumping aloud. "Jessica!" she called out. Getting no response, she wanted to run after her but she quickly checked herself. A body had already been dropped in the woods; she didn't want to add hers to the count. "I said I was sorry!" she said, pleading. As she watched Jessica leave, she stretched her hand forward, pleading and crying profusely. Jessica ignored her completely, not even honoring her with a backward glance.

Standing alone in the middle of the woods, Mikayla stamped her foot against the ground several times in anguish. After reality had set in, she decided she had only one option left—to keep on moving. Making up her mind, Mikayla began walking down the dirt path where Jessica had disappeared ahead a few minutes earlier. As she trekked on, the farther she got, the narrower the path became, with bushes and shrubs closing in on both sides of the road.

She felt irritated as the grasses brushed against her legs and she bent down to brush it off. Suddenly, she heard a twig snap closely behind her. Mikayla quickly stood upright and whirled around. "Mitch? Keith? Is that you?" she called out, her eyes wide from fright. There was no one in sight. "If this is one of your sick games, Mitch, let me be. I'm in no mood for it," she shouted again.

Mikayla had half-expected Mitch to jump out from behind a shrub, laughing maniacally and delivering one of his lame punch lines. However, she was met with utter silence, which soon began to unnerve her. Mikayla waited for about a minute for someone to show up. When nothing moved, she gave up waiting and turned around to resume her trek, feeling slightly annoyed by the unnecessary disturbance that delayed her. As she turned, the color drained from her face at the sight before her. Standing directly in front of her was Danny, wearing a black hood. Out of fear, Mikayla's heart skipped several beats. Tears began to well up in her eyes. Her breath got heavier, and she started hyperventilating as she panicked. "Please, Danny. I'm sorry," she whimpered like a shriveled rat.

In response, Danny smiled and took a step toward her, his intentions well hidden behind the dark eyes.

Jessica continued to stomp down the path with heavy footsteps. She was seething with rage; she blamed Mikayla for betraying her and herself for trusting the two-timing bitch with the secret of her affection for Danny in the first place. If she hadn't shared her location with her so-called friend, then none of this would've happened and Danny would still be here.

As she rebuked herself in various ways for her poor choice of companionship, a shriek pierced the air. Even if Jessica's thoughts weren't dwelling on her already, she could easily recognize Mikayla's low-pitched voice anywhere. Jessica stopped and waited to listen more attentively. Again, the shriek rang through the air, and this time, Jessica realized that it was her name being called in what seemed like a desperate cry for help.

She wondered if this was a ploy by Mikayla to get her attention or if indeed she was in danger. None of the scenarios playing in her head appealed to her emotionally; she really didn't care much anymore. Jessica kept a virtual trash can in her head where she segregated the people who had wronged her, making her keep the relationship she had with those people to a bare minimum. Fresh at the top of the dump files was Mikayla, her friend who had stabbed her in the back and cost her dearly.

Now, hearing her cries for help, Jessica was torn between ignoring her and coming to her rescue. If the threat was a big one, why should she put herself in harm's way for a traitor? Jessica's thoughts spiraled widely as she thought of the different ways this could end. Just then, Mikayla yelled her name again, pleading for help in a teary voice. This seemed to make the decision for her; without any further delay, Jessica turned around and began running up the dirt path she had just come from.

After running for several minutes, she couldn't trace the origin of the noise as it seemed to be coming from all around her. She was momentarily lost in the forest.

Meanwhile, Mikayla was screaming loudly and weeping, the ground beneath her wet with tears. She was kicking her leg frantically at Danny, who was unfazed as she tried to crawl away, digging her manicured fingers into the dirt.

Danny pulled her by the waist and flipped her on her back. Mikayla looked truly petrified, turning as white as a ghost. "Please. Don't hurt me," she pleaded, sobbing.

Danny shook his head, unforgiving. He knelt down and placed his palms around her neck. Mikayla gasped for air as he began to choke her. The earth beneath them started shaking and from it sprouted roots the color of soot, coiling around Danny from his waist up to his torso and then his outstretched arms, crawling down his sleeves. The roots began twisting around Mikayla's neck, intertwining with each other as they tightened slowly, making a dull fastening noise. She tried to open her mouth to breathe but the air supply had been completely cut from her lungs. Mikayla's eyes bulged out, nearly popping out of her skull. A slow wheeze began escaping from her mouth.

Suddenly, Danny let go of his hold on her, losing concentration as a dazed expression showed on his face. Mikayla was no longer there, his mother momentarily took her place staring at him with no expression. Distracted by what could have been a message, the thick twigs began to retract back into the ground.

Seeing an opportunity to escape, Mikayla jumped up and ran in Jessica's direction. As she wailed and made to run past her, Jessica grabbed her and pulled her into her arms. "What's going on, Mikky?" she asked, puzzled.

Mikayla tried to speak but the words couldn't escape her sore throat. She began to gasp. Jessica quickly placed a hand on her chest and ran it up and down in an attempt to pacify her.

After she had calmed a little, Mikayla leaned forward, placing her hands on her knees, sighing heavily in quick succession to catch her breath.

"Are you okay?" Jessica asked, looking genuinely concerned about her.

Mikayla shook her head furiously and swallowed hard a few times, her breathing still audible. "No, I'm not okay. He was there, he was there..." she stated, pointing to the spot where she had just left.

"What? Who was there?" Jessica asked, confused.

"Danny... Danny was there. I'm sorry, I'm so sorry," Mikayla replied, sounding hysterical.

Jessica looked bewildered, trying to put the pieces together. She couldn't make much sense of what was going on, no matter how much she tried. As she stared at Mikayla's red eyeballs and bruised neck, she was surprised to hear that it was Danny attempting to kill her. Had his death turn him into a vengeful, murderous spirit? Endless questions filled her mind as she tried to make sense of the situation. To her, it seemed like Danny's ghost was coming for the people who killed him. A chilling sensation passed through her spine as she wondered if his spirit considered her as an accomplice to the murder. After all, she was present at the scene and had watched helplessly as Gill and his friends connived to leave him in the woods for dead. Moreover, she hadn't said anything to anyone since about it. Why hadn't she contacted the police? This train of thought made her head ache as she realized she might not be safe after all.

Jessica glanced sideways at Mikayla, who looked so petrified, as if she had come face to face with the grim reaper himself.

Mikayla's hair was badly ruffled and dirty. However, her looks were the least of her concern at that moment. All she wanted to do was get out of that God-forsaken forest alive.

Jessica started at the red welts which were beginning to appear at Mikayla's neck. Just then, a whooshing noise pierced the air once again. Jessica's eyes roamed the surroundings, dread slowly creeping into her heart. "We need to get out of here now!" she said with great urgency.

Mikayla swallowed hard once again and nodded approvingly.

Officer Teresa's nose was upturned as she stepped out of the school's bathroom. After all her years in service, she had never seen a crime scene as gory as the one in the room she had just left. Teresa pulled off her medical gloves, specifically made for situations just like this.

A yellow tape was used to barricade the hall at both ends, barricading the area around the bathroom. Crime scene investigators and police officers walked about, going in and out of the bathroom, hurriedly trying to clean up the mess and preserve evidence. Teresa looked around with focused eyes, scrutinizing the environment as she tried to figure out what exactly had happened.

As she stood in the hallway, she saw Doug coming toward her. He crouched to pass beneath the yellow tape, his back touching the thin nylon, making it stretch as if it would snap.

"Typical Doug. Clumsy, little guy," Teresa muttered under her breath.

As Doug got clear of the demarcation, he glanced back at it, amusement on his face as if he had just overcome a monumental hurdle. After a few seconds, he turned around and began to approach Teresa. He glanced into the bloody bathroom from over her shoulder. Getting a glimpse of the scene inside, he ran his hand through his hair and whistled. "Talk about a mess, huh?"

Teresa nodded absentmindedly. "Yeah. Were there any witnesses?" she asked.

Doug shook his head, a sad puppy look in his eyes. "I checked with Principal Red, there were no witnesses. Although, a teacher mentioned that the boy was acting unusually strange in class and had bolted out earlier just moments before..." Doug completed his sentence by nodding his head toward the bathroom.

Teresa looked deep in thought as she considered the words of her fellow officer for a minute. Then she said, "Get me a list of all of his closest friends."

"On it," Doug responded. He threw her a mock salute, smirking before turning around and leaving.

As Teresa watched him walk down the hall toward the staff room, the single thought in her head was solving the mystery of this disturbing murder. Someone had to have known something, she told herself as she looked over at the swarm of students gathered at end of the hallway, watching the authorities work from afar. As her eyes roamed the innocent- looking faces of the students, she spotted a face that was out of place.

Standing a good foot above most of the students was a man in his late forties with tears in his eyes. She studied him for a minute, taking in all she could. From his appearance, she came to a gut-wrenching conclusion— the man was the father of Gill, the dead boy in the bathroom. Their resemblance was uncanny, with the same bulky body structure, hair type and color, as well as their facial features.

As she thought about what to do, the man looked her way and caught her staring at him. Teresa could feel part of the man's sorrow from his defeated gait; it was an inconsolable pain, losing one's child. With sadness in her heart, Teresa began walking toward the man, thinking of the right words to say in this kind of situation.

The local super store was scantily crowded that day. It was the go-to place for all everyone's needs, and it was frequented by most people in town. The subtly-named Dre-Mart Mega Store offered groceries, electrical equipment, computers and hardware accessories, household goods and equipment, clothes, as well as a small music section at a corner of the giant store.

At one of the checkout points, a cashier placed a torch, a gas tank, gloves, and a can of WD-40 on the counter. The cashier, a young man in his mid-to-late thirties with a handsome face which had undoubtedly seen better days, stared at the two customers before him from behind wide-rimmed glasses, and then looked back at the items on the table. With a puzzled look in his eyes, he smiled nervously and slid the products down the cash register.

Mitch nodded curtly at the man as he gathered some of their purchased items in his hands while Keith, who stood behind them, stepped forward to help with the rest. Together, they turned around and left the store with their merchandise of death in their arms.

The setting sun cast a beautiful, yellow hue on the vegetation, giving the atmosphere a surreal, cinematic feel. *It isn't all so bad out here*, Danny thought. He was on his back, lying on grasses deep in Witch's Creek. All around him were nothing but trees, animals, and the best of nature. Ever since his transformation, Danny had been spending most of his time in the forest. Being a lone wolf for most of his life, now he had grown to prefer the comfort of wildlife to humans. Animals were easy to understand and relate with—all you need is to feed them and build a connection with them. Regardless how ferocious that beast may be regarded, it will remain loyal to you for life. Humans on the other hand, were manipulative, evil, and murderous creatures; something he had gotten to learn at a grave price. Even the ones you call friends may not come to your aid when you need them, he told himself as images of Jessica's smile came to mind.

Danny stared up at the sky, watching as the sun slowly went to rest for the day, changing shifts to illuminate the path of others in another part of the world. The moon crept up slowly from a corner of the sky, happy that its rival had once again relinquished control of the skies to it. The moon began to glow triumphantly, beckoning to its brethren, the stars, to come shine light on the night together, as tiny sparkling dots began to appear in the sky.

Danny sighed contentedly from where he lay as his heart glowed warmly, grateful for witnessing the beautiful act of power changing hands in the blue sky, which had now turned a hundred shades darker, just like his soul.

Danny's thoughts drifted to a time long ago, before the proverbial shit hit the fan, splattering his life with permanent filth.

14 Years Ago

"Please, David. Don't do this!" Elinore pleaded. She was on her knees, and her hands were clenching the edge of her husband's shirt tightly.

"Get your damn paws off me, woman!" David shouted. He tried to wriggle himself from her grip, unsuccessfully. He chose the quicker and meaner route and pushed her to the ground.

From the window of the backseat of the truck, seven-year-old Danny watched his parents argue. He sat patiently in the car, wondering what had gone wrong this time. Over the past year, his mother and father had been having little spats and arguments, which they often tried to shield from him. However, Danny noticed that in the past month, his dad had been drinking more heavily, and with it, his parents' fights had also gotten louder and more violent. Sometimes he felt like running to them to make them stop yelling at each other, but he knew better than to get in the middle of their fights. They'd seemed to work it out and act lovingly to each other, well, until their next fight and everything turned upside down again.

From the window, Danny watched as his father took a swig from the beer bottle in his hand, draining the content of the glass bottle before tossing it aside.

"Please. Stop, David! Stop!" Elinore begged from where she lay on the dirty ground. Ignoring his wife's pleas, David began to walk toward the truck, his legs slightly shaky. As he stumbled to the driver's door, he looked down into the back-seat at Danny, who kept his eyes straight ahead, before entering the car. David glanced at his wife, who was just starting to stand up. "Get inside now!" he ordered in a deep voice.

Elinore ran up to the truck and rode shotgun, all the while pleading to her husband to hearken to her voice of reasoning. As vehemently as she pleaded, she was equally dismissed.

Seeing her efforts were futile, Elinore glanced back at Danny, silently wondering if they weren't already damaging the kid with their incessant arguments and fights. It wasn't her fault, she told herself, her husband had just grown to be an inattentive, stubborn goat, with the situation made worse by his excessive drinking.

The mother stared at her son affectionately, silently apologizing for all the troubles they were putting him through. She reached out slowly and touched his neatly-combed, black hair. "Danny," she said, her voice carrying all her emotions in that single word.

"Mom…" Danny said as a black tear rolled down his cheek. All around the ground around him, thick, dark roots had grown, some of them wrapping the lower parts of his body. Noticing he had used his powers subconsciously, he opened his eyes and used his mind to control the roots and force them back into the ground.

He looked around the forest, taking in the beautiful scenery. It was much brighter than when he had closed his eyes. As a ray of light caught his eyes from above, he realized it was daybreak already.

Danny pulled out a hoodie from the bag he had grown to take everywhere he went now. It was his emergency tool bag which contained his essentials. It came in very handy.

He wore the jacket and pulled down his sleeves to cover his arms before draping the hoodie over his head. His face was well obscured, and unless he pulled off the hoodie in public anyone who looked at his darkened face could easily chuck him up as a Goth kid who took his art too far.

Well-disguised, Danny flung his bag over his shoulder and began his journey out of the forest.

Officer Teresa sat quietly behind the wheels of her cop car as she drove around town. She was on patrol but so far, it had been a relatively quiet day. It was evening already, and the only major crime that had been reported all day was about graffiti painting. When she had grudgingly drove to the location, the teenagers dispersed and ran away as soon as they saw her approaching.

She hadn't bothered to chase after any of them; bigger things occupied her mind than a bunch of kids painting the sigil of Superman on the side wall of a warehouse.

Teresa had turned around and gotten into her car. "The situation has been handled," she had called in, as she turned around and began driving toward the more populated part of town where most of the crimes occurred.

As she drove down a quiet street, she noticed two boys walking close to each other on the sidewalk. The boys were carrying big, white bags and they were looking around and over their shoulders as if they were wary of being followed. Officer Teresa became suspicious so she began driving toward them.

Keith was the first to notice the police car approaching them from behind.

"Shit, shit! Cop car!" he said, growing more nervous.

Mitch didn't bother to glance around as he presumed it may tick off the officer that they were up to something.

"Shut up and act normal," he stated, glancing at Keith out of the corner of his eyes.

"I'm calm!" Keith said.

"Then shut the fuck up!" Mitch retorted, gritting his teeth as he spoke so as not to raise his voice.

The car pulled up beside them, and they both stopped in their tracks.

"Evening, boys," Teresa called out from the driver's seat, winding down the window of the passenger's door.

"Evening ma'am," Keith and Mitch responded together. Teresa craned her neck to get a clearer view of them. "Whatcha up to?"

Keith tried to hide the bag behind his back. Neither he nor his friend responded to the officer's question.

Undeterred, Teresa persisted. "Hardware store? Project?" she suggested. "Yeah!" Keith quickly replied, jumping at the lifeline.

Mitch glanced sideways at him and rolled his eyes. Then, he turned back to face the police officer to say, "Yeah. We... Gill was our friend, and we are doing something for him. We wanted to make him and his family something after the horrible thing that happened." Although, he looked truly dejected, his voice didn't carry any of the tenderness in the words he uttered.

"Oh, I'm sorry about that," Teresa replied.

"Thanks, ma'am... Do you have an idea what exactly happened?" Keith said.

"Hmm... not yet. I'm sorry, boys, but we are still trying to get to the bottom of this." The boys nodded, hoping to be let off soon.

Teresa smiled briefly and took a few seconds to think. Out of nowhere, she asked in a casual tone, "Say, you haven't seen Danny anywhere lately have you?"

"No, no, not at all," Keith blurted, shaking his head vigorously.

Mitch threw him a dangerous look. He looked back at the cop and in a more composed manner, he stated, "No. Actually, last time we saw him was at school a couple of days ago."

Teresa nodded in understanding. "As Gill's close friends, I know you boys like to tease him..." She paused and noticed the boys' discomfort at what she said. However, she didn't read much into their uneasiness—she assumed they were growing bored of the conversation already. She finished her sentence, saying, "Be easy on him, he's been through a lot."

Mitch stared at her and smiled, the warmth not reaching his piercing, cold eyes.

"Be good, boys. Play nice," Teresa said. With that, she started up the car and drove off.

The boys watched the car go. "Wow. That was close," Keith said, letting out a long sigh as beads of sweat rolled off his face.

Mitch gave him no response. As soon as the police car disappeared out of sight, he dropped the bag he held on the sidewalk. Suddenly, he grabbed his friend by the collar and pushed him into an alley very close by, slamming his back against a wall.

"What's wrong with you, man?" Keith yelled as he unsuccessfully attempted to snatch himself out of his grasp.

"You need to stop fucking around," Mitch stated coldly. His face was screwed up tight in anger.

Keith looked bewildered, wondering what had come over his friend. "Get the fuck off me now!" he shouted, tugging at his collar in his grip.

Mitch leaned against him and pushed him harder into the wall. He put his hand into his jacket's inner pocket and pulled out an item.

Keith's eyes widened with fear and confusion as he heard the unmistakable sound of a switch blade being flicked open. He went silent as he saw the dirty blade of the knife being held up to his face.

"See that, huh? That's the blood of that little bitch," Mitch stated, his mouth moving rapidly as if he was a snake spitting venom.

Keith didn't utter a single word as his eyes remained glued to the knife, wondering if his blood was about to be spilled next by the blade.

Speaking more slowly, Mitch said, "I'm not going under for him…" Drawing out each word slowly to hammer home his point, he continued, "We are going to finish this off and forget it ever happened." He slowly glided the knife across Keith's letterman jacket, the blade's point slightly pushing into his chest. "You, with your pretty mug and hot body will be going off to college with your fancy scholarships… Live a perfect life," he said, his voice growing lower and lower as he uttered each word until the last one was said just above a whisper.

As he spoke, he stood face to face with Keith, leaning in closely. Suddenly, he brought down his lips on his friend's, kissing him slowly. Surprisingly, Keith didn't protest. Instead, he parted his lips slightly for a passionate bout of kissing.

As the lip locking grew more intense, Keith began to giggle. He shoved Mitch backward and they both began to laugh. "Prick," he said, shoving his friend once again. Mitch shoved him back and soon they were chasing each other around the alley, cackling aloud in excitement.

6

ALL AT ONCE

The evening was unusually quiet at Jessica's house. At that time of the day, she was usually hooked to the screen of their television or her laptop, watching her favorite comedy shows. If she was engaged in other activities, she would be busy belting out Jon Bellion's tunes from her music player.

However, none of that was happening today. Jessica sat idly at the edge of the bed, watching Mikayla sleep, her hair falling perfectly on her face as she looked so peaceful. It had taken great effort to calm her, and when her hysteria was getting out of hand, Jessica had to bring her to her home and slipped a little dose of her sleeping pill into the beverage she made for her, just so she could get some sleep.

Jessica herself wasn't feeling too great. The thoughts running through her mind had left her mentally exhausted, and she feared she was very close to having a nervous breakdown. She began to sob, cursing her stars for getting her involved in the fight between the boys, which was starting to push her to the edge of her sanity.

Suddenly, the bedroom door creaked and Jessica quickly shifted where she sat as she tried to regain her composure.

Her father stuck his head through the door and looked around. "You guys okay?" he asked.

"Yes, Dad," she responded in a cracked voice, sniffling as she uttered each word. She looked down and nodded in affirmation.

Sensing her sadness, Oliver walked into the room and placed a hand on her shoulder. "Honey, what's wrong?"

Jessica's sobs grew louder as she felt her father's comforting touch. She and the man were close when she was younger, forming a strong bond between each other. She used to open up to him about everything that went on in her life. However, as she grew older, she kept more to herself, and the connection she had with her father became weakened as they drifted apart. Still, she knew the man always had her best interests at heart, even though his decisions could seem harsh to outsiders.

Jessica looked up at her father, wondering if she could trust him with the secret that was burning a hole in her heart. Her options weren't many and she knew she could be putting herself in harm's way if she didn't reach out to someone soon for help. As she stared into her father's face, she noticed the tender look of concern that floated in his eyes; who better to pour her heart out to than the man who could protect her with his life, she thought. Summoning up courage, Jessica said, "Dad, we did something... Something very terrible."

"Honey, what happened? Did someone hurt you?" Oliver asked. Never taking his hand off her shoulder, he sat down beside her on the bed.

Jessica burst into tears, shaking her head vehemently. "No, Dad. We... We killed someone..."

The man jumped to his feet and stood before his daughter to get a clear view of her face. "What do you mean 'killed?'"

Jessica began stammering as blurted out some incomprehensible jargon. Finally, she caught her breath and in a slower tone, she said, "He died... but he didn't stay dead."

Oliver looked puzzled and dazed as he pondered the gravity of his daughter's words.

Days Of Our Lives is becoming a boring show these days, Teresa thought as she watched the TV absent-mindedly. She had grown up watching the show with her family, cultivating a sort of cult-following for the soap opera. Teresa had carried the family torch through the years and had remained a loyal fan of the show. However, probably due to production changes made in the past couple of seasons, the show had become cheesy and drab. Common sense was beginning to overrule family traditions as she was starting to lose interest in the show; something none of her family members should hear about, lest she risk being disowned.

Teresa had turned down the lights in the room, hoping to improve the viewing experience with a cinematic atmosphere, but it didn't help much. She tried to focus on the background story, ignoring the corny dialogue as she waited for the whistle of the kettle. She had been craving homemade tea and once she had gotten home and changed into a skimpy, white nightgown, she had quickly gone to make preparations for the beverage. Now, she watered her mouth in anticipation as she watched the television show.

Suddenly, Teresa cocked her ears as she heard the sound of knuckles rapping against the front door. She stood up from the couch and walked the short distance to the door. She peered outside through the eye hole and saw a hooded person standing outside, holding a bunch of red flowers. Although she couldn't see the person's face, she could tell from his stature that it was Danny. Besides, he was the only person she was in a romantic relationship with at present and it would be weird if anyone else came to her house with flowers.

Teresa opened the door and stood by the entrance. She took in his look—the dark clothes and shrouded face. Her sixth sense was telling her that something was off.

Danny stretched out his hand and handed her the flowers. As Teresa collected them, she noticed dirt in their roots. She could tell that he had uprooted them by himself; she wondered where he had found the flowers as she smiled nervously and said her thanks.

"May I come in?" Danny asked.

"Sure," she responded, stepping out of the way to let him in. Danny took the invitation and passed by her as she locked the door behind him.

As soon as he heard the bolting sound of the lock, Danny grabbed Teresa by the shoulder and whirled her around. Facing her, he kissed her on the lips before she could get a word out. They knocked each other around the room until they had made their way to the kitchen.

Danny lifted her and placed her butt on the counter with ease. The dim ambience of the room made the atmosphere more romantic. Danny moved his lips away from hers and began kissing down her neck, eliciting gasps from her.

As Teresa moaned in pleasure, she caught a glimpse of dark veins at the back of his hands. This momentarily broke her out of her reverie. "Danny...?" she called out in a low voice.

Mistaking her call as an act of pleasure, he increased the pace of the kisses as his hand began rubbing her bare thigh inward.

Teresa was caught in the deep throes of passion as she moaned louder at his touch.

She didn't make any attempt to stop him.

Danny flipped her over, making her face the stove where the water was beginning to make boiling noises. He pulled up her soft lingerie, feeling the silk in his palm before he pulled down his pants and drove inside.

"Uhhh," Teresa moaned as she felt the heat of passion.

She held on for dear life, unwilling to let go of him. His shoulders were so strong, rippling with muscles beneath his clothes. The way he grunted with each pump inside of her left her breathless and she was hanging on by a thin thread.

Danny grunted heavily and after a few more thrusts, he let it all out and crashed onto her.

Teresa tried to wriggle out from under him with difficulty as she was beginning to feel suffocated as her chest pressed against the counter.

Finally, she was able to pull down her clothing as Danny craned his neck, planting soft kisses all over the area that was accessible to him.

Teresa started to feel snugly, and she turned her head sideways to give him more access to her neck. However, what laid in her sight was unexpectedly horrifying— while Danny rested on her, his palm was on the stove, having displaced the kettle.

Teresa jolted upright as she yelled, "Danny! Danny! Danny! Your hand!"

Danny took a step back and looked around, wondering what was going on. He was seemingly oblivious of his hand on the stove, which had already began to smoke like a piece of wood.

Dazed by confusion, Teresa was mute, and all she could was point at his burning hand.

Danny stared down at it and an "oh" look crossed his face. He stood still for a few seconds, contemplating what to do. Coming to a decision, he suddenly pulled up his pants hurriedly and ran out the front door, leaving a more confused Teresa behind, alone.

⁕

The mobile home stood alone at the edge of town, surrounded by forest like an island in the middle of an ocean. Everywhere was quiet, and no light was coming from inside the house. An outsider would've presumed no one home. However, that wasn't Mitch's prayer, as he hoped to catch Danny inside.

A few feet away from the porch, he stood holding a bottle of molotov cocktail in his hand. Mitch trained his eyes on the sitting room window, aiming. He couldn't afford to miss, he told himself. After taking a deep breath, he threw the homemade explosive.

The sound of glass cracking echoed all around as the bottle cracked the window and smashed to the living room floor. Mitch could see licks of fire splattering around inside the house. He smiled in excitement, controlling the urge to jump up and throw his fist in the air triumphantly.

"Let's get out of here now," Keith called out from behind him.

"No, just a while longer. Don't deny me this pleasure," Mitch replied, a wide maniacal grin creeping across his face.

From inside the house, Zeus began to growl as the glass smashed and the fire began to spread. Beneath the front door and through the broken window, smoke began to curl out. The fire caught the drapes in the living room, licking at its edge gently before growing fiercer and beginning to engulf it.

The Doberman started barking wildly, pounding on the door and scratching the wood with its nails.

As Mitch heard the barks of a dog coming from inside, he became more thrilled. "Light up the second one!" he ordered.

A minute later, Keith was holding a flaming bottle of Molotov cocktail in his hand. He threw it at another window—unbeknownst to him, it was Danny's bedroom—and watched it smash inside forcefully. "Whoo!" he shouted, pumping his fist in the air at his perfect shot.

Zeus began pounding harder against the door, rattling the locked chain that held it in place. The dog struggled to escape from the burning house but his efforts proved futile.

Meanwhile, the two boys stood outside at a safe distance, watching their work of destruction in awe. The dancing flames reflected in their starry eyes, making them look like hypnotized mental patients. They stood rooted to the spot they were on, unmoving, except for their eyes darting around to take in every minute of the arson.

Sensing there was no way to get past the door without help, Zeus began pacing. He navigated to where David sat quietly on the couch. Zeus began tugging at the edge of the man's trousers, wondering if he had fell into one of his stupors. However, David's eyes were wide open and he saw the house burning but he made no attempt to move.

Meanwhile, Mitch and Keith were outside, enthralled, waiting to hear a sound of human activity coming from inside. Mitch silently hoped to smoke Danny out of the front door; he wanted to gut him again, this time, finishing off the work.

However, after several minutes, nobody came out through the door, and the fire had already begun to rage harder, spreading to other parts of the house. "Let's leave now," Mitch stated, feeling a pang of disappointment as he didn't get to fulfill his silent wish—killing Danny with his own hands.

He straightened his jacket before he and his friend raced off. They had only ran a few paces when Mitch's switchblade slipped and fell from his pocket, unnoticed, stabbing the ground. The boys soon disappeared around the corner of the road, leaving the house burning wildly behind.

Inside the mobile home, Zeus still ran frantically about in an attempt to escape. The fire had consumed the windows, and most of the house was on fire by then.

David got up from where he sat. He began navigating through the flames, and Zeus followed him closely, the Doberman's hope of freedom nearly close to realization. However, rather than going in the direction of the door, David made a left turn and walked up to a table. On it were stacks of books and also scattered around on the surface were receipts, flyers, and photos. The fire hadn't touched the table yet but it was already getting closer.

David picked up a framed picture and looked at it. Staring back at him with beautiful smiles on their faces were Elinore and Danny. *Indeed, there have been simpler days,* he thought, his head flooding with images of everything he had lost.

After taking a long look at the photo of a better time from the past, he placed the picture back on the table. Tears rolled down his cheeks as he turned around and took in the inferno raging right before his eyes, a small taste of the hell he was about to visit.

The dog saw the fear in the man's eyes; it was a reflection of the one in his tinier ones.

Zeus lay down at his feet, snuggling up to him in resignation to his fate.

David crouched and placed his hand on the dog's head. For the first time, he looked at the Doberman affectionately. "It will be over soon," he said, patting the dog as the flames intensified all around them.

⁓

Danny sprinted through the forest at rocket speed for about thirty minutes, not once stopping to catch his breath. Although the evening light was very low, he was able to navigate through the woods with ease, partly because his eyes had grown accustomed to the darkness and also because he had grown familiar with the forest around his house as he had been going there for several years.

However, as Danny ran through the forest that day, something felt very off. He was firstly ticked off when he felt a flake landing on his shoulder. He was surprised as it wasn't winter yet and it hadn't been snowing lately. When he touched the flake, he realized it was ashes. Just then, he looked up ahead and noticed that afar, thick smoke was rising up to the sky.

What asshole could be burning the forest, didn't they know people lived close by? He began to run faster.

As Danny came to a clearing, he pumped the breaks of his feet. His eyes widened in shock and horror as realization dawned on him that the flaming edifice was his home. He ran to the front door and cracked it down with a kick. Smoke and flames blew out at him, excited by the new outlet and supply of oxygen.

Danny stepped into the house, unfazed and unharmed by the fires. He looked around in anger; the house had nearly been completely engulfed. Parts of the roof had caved in, crashing upon various items around.

His vision was blurred by the smoke, and he couldn't make out much in the room. He focused his eyes and soon enough, he noticed his father and Zeus laying on the floor by the table. Danny quickly rushed to them.

He knelt beside them and saw parts of his father's legs and chest had been badly burnt. Danny felt for his pulse and let out a slow sigh of relief when he found the veins still throbbing. He quickly crouched up to Zeus, who lay unmoving. Pain filled his guts as he tried to shake the dog awake but couldn't.

Instantly, he picked up the large Doberman's lifeless body and grabbed Davids foot. As he began dragging David and carrying Zeus outside, he felt a tug. A groan from behind him made him turn around. Danny saw that his father was staring at him, holding the tables leg. He looked at him, and their eyes met, lingering for a moment. Then, the older man smiled and gave him a gentle nod, the latter of which was reciprocated as Danny gently placed his foot down. With the silent message passed between them, Danny stepped out through the doorless front entrance.

Walking several paces away from the burning house, Danny lay the dog down on the grass. Danny placed his hand on Zeus and concentrated his powers on bringing his loyal companion back to life. His palm began glowing brightly as he transferred part of his energy into the dog.

After a few attempts, Zeus let out quick short breaths, wheezing slightly. Danny retracted his hand as energy had nearly been depleted by the reanimation process; he crashed down and placed his head on the dog's midsection.

He began to tremble as he cried. Tears dropped from his eyes, clear liquid the dark shade of night. The tears dropped onto Zeus's fur, steaming off of the dog's already burnt skin. The Doberman began to growl, his eyes darting around menacingly.

From where he lay, Danny was overwhelmed with emotions, and he let out a mighty roar.

The truck barreled down the deserted highway at high speed. The tires skidded as David made a sharp turn, an exhilarated look crossing his face. "David! Please pull over. I beg of you," Elinore urged.

"Shut up, woman. I know what I'm doing," David retorted. His eyes drooped for a second, and the truck lost balance as it began swerving across both lanes.

Elinore quickly extended her hand to grab the steering and correct the movement. At that moment, David jolted awake. Anticipating his wife's move, he smacked her face, and she sat back down.

Instantly, Elinore's hand went to her cheek as she tried to rub off the stinging pain. "David, what the hell? You are going to kill us all," she shouted.

David ignored her as he kept a hand on the wheel while he scratched his belly with the other.

Elinore glanced back to look at the third occupant of the vehicle—her son, Danny, who sat quietly in backseat. She noticed his seat belt wasn't clicked in; she reached out to buckle him in.

Just then, David's eyes began to droop as the alcohol kicked into his system. He shut his eyes momentarily and let go of his grip on the steering wheel. He swerved off the road and lost control. "Shit!" he muttered as he jolted back awake, a few seconds too late.

As the truck nearly hit a tall tree by the side of the road, Danny yelled, "Mommy!"

"What's it?" Elinore said as she locked in her son's seatbelt, sat back, and looked forward just in time for the heavy collision.

The truck jerked back and forth, and the force of the collision sent the unbuckled woman flying out through the windshield and into the night.

In the darkness, dazed, young Danny could hear the sound of his mother smacking hard into a tree, the noise of breaking bones audible, before Elinore flopped down, dead.

The small diner was dimly-lit, with the exception of smoke coming from the kitchen.

There were only about eight tables in the place, with two short benches attached to each table at both sides.

Mitch and Keith sat at one of these benches, grinning heartily at each other. A young waiter walked up to them and placed two plates on the table before them. The young girl was about their age, with curly, blonde hair, pretty, bright eyes, dimpled cheeks, and a stud gold nose ring; she sure was a true beauty.

"Cheerios for you, and... eggs n' hash browns for you," she said, nodding politely.

Mitch stared at the name on her chest tag and smiled at her. "Thank you, Debbie," he said.

Debbie smiled coyly and winked at the boys before she walked off. Mitch kept his eyes glued to her jiggling ass in the tight jeans before she disappeared behind the counter and entered the kitchen.

As she walked into the room and closed the door behind her, she saw Alvaro inside flipping and scraping eggs as the oil sizzled. The heat was making the chef sweat slightly. Debbie picked up a rag and walked up to him to wipe his face with it.

"Thanks, darling," Alvaro said. His head was full of long, thick hair, which made him look much younger than the forty-two-year-old man he was. However, the dampness in the room had made his hair greasy, but he didn't seem to mind much.

Debbie watched him for a few seconds, admiring the man's commitment to his work. Although Alvaro was undeniably a handsome man and they had a good rapport, their relationship was more like a father-daughter bond. She respected the man very much, and she often wondered if she would've made a pass at him if he were a few decades younger. However, she liked the way they were, and besides, he wasn't really the type of guy she often went out with. Debbie had a taste for the wild ones; she wasn't a fan of long-term commitments.

"I'm going out for a smoke, Alvaro," she said. "Alright. It's fine," the chef responded.

As she passed by him, Debbie smacked his ass, running the rest of the short distance to the back door.

Debbie closed the door behind her with a bang and stepped out into the open air.

The diner's location was isolated with the nearest building still a long way away. A major road passed through the front of the diner, and the backyard was nothing but open space. The only object in the surrounding was a giant dumpster which was placed against a corner wall at the back of the diner.

Debbie stood a few paces away from the door before she lit her cigarette. She took a long drag of it and let out the smoke slowly, sighing in relief as the tension built up in her body began to seep away. Although, the night was brightly lit by the moon, she didn't care much about it or the stars. The aesthetic of nature was lost to her. The only thought that was on her mind was to finish smoking on time so she could go back inside, work, and rake in more tips before her shift was over.

As she enjoyed the peace and comfort the cigarette gave her, she heard a voice call out, "Can I have a smoke?"

Startled, Debbie whirled around quickly enough to see Mitch appearing from behind the dumpster. He began to approach her. Debbie was a little bit freaked out, but she tried to maintain her calm. "Sure, you can take a smoke," she responded, shrugging casually.

She stretched out her hand to give him the cigarette stick. Suddenly, Mitch grabbed her by the wrist and roughly pulled her closer.

"Let go of me," Debbie snarled. She tried to wriggle her hand out of his grasp but she couldn't.

Mitch stared at her amusingly. "Can I have a kiss?" he said in a tone that was meant to be seductive but was simply irritating.

"I said let go now!" Debbie replied, raising her voice a few notches in anger. She tried to push him away, but he tightened his grip on her wrist.

Suddenly, Mitch shoved her against the dumpster with her back to him. He began to fumble at her pant button as he attempted to pull it with his free hand while the other pressed against her back.

"Stop! No-no-no... please don't do this," she pleaded, crying out loud. Putting all her strength into her back, she tried to shove him off of her.

Mitch was having none of that; he smacked her across the face. "Shut up, slut!" he said in a hushed tone.

Still, she kicked at him with the back of her legs and tried to wriggle away. Mitch was angered as she moved about, making it difficult for him to have his way with her. "Stay still, bitch," he snapped with a hint of warning in his voice.

As he raised his hand to slap her again, he was stopped midair. Mitch was surprised that someone had dared to stop him. However, before he could turn around to see who it was, a powerful hand grabbed him by the shoulder and slammed him back against the dumpster next to Debbie. Mitch bent over as he groaned in pain.

Debbie looked up at the darkened, scary face of her savior. "Leave, now..." Danny said to her.

She didn't wait a second longer as she hurried away, walking a few steps before she broke into a sprint and ran into the diner through the back door.

Mitch had regained his composure, and he stood straight before Danny. "You little bitch. I've dealt with your ass once; you think I'm afraid of you now?" he spewed rapidly.

Danny stared back at him, the hoodie still draped over his head.

Mitch hesitated before attacking; he wanted to analyze what he was up against first. Even though Danny's face was covered by his hoodie, he could still notice some dark lines running all over his face. Also, he seemed to have grown more muscular as he could make out his bulging biceps which strained his sweater. *So what, he had been working out? I can still hand him his ass, this time finishing him off for real*, Mitch told himself. However, he knew Danny would be at an advantage if he made the first attack; he needed to goad the nerd into making a move. Out loud, he said, "How's your dog?"

Infuriated, Danny took two menacing steps forward, closing the gap between them. Mitch sidestepped and grabbed him by the collar. With all his energy, he attempted to throw him away but he didn't budge an inch.

Danny's head was hung low. Dramatically, he slowly raised his head up and stared Mitch in the eyes. Mitch was caught off guard and was disoriented as he looked into those black, glassy eyes. They seemed to be beckoning him to come closer, to jump in and swim in the bottomless ocean.

Before he could break out of the hypnotic hold, Danny grabbed him by the wrists. Mitch watched helplessly as a smirk appeared at the corner of Danny's mouth. Just then, very slowly and methodically, Danny began to twist his wrists around. He didn't stop when he heard the cracking sound of bones breaking.

"Ah-ah, fuck you. Ahhh," Mitch cried out, spitting between clenched teeth as he felt excruciating pain.

Finally, Danny released his hold on him after he had made a complete one-eighty degree and Mitch's palms were now facing him.

Just then, the back door of the diner opened and Chef Alvaro walked out just in time to see Mitch's hands turned backward before they dropped and began flopping around as there was no longer bone support at the wrist. Debbie had initially informed him that a pervert had attempted to rape her outside but a scary young man had come to her rescue. He hadn't come out to check earlier as he had an urgent order to attend to and he had figured that the creep would've run away already. However, as he had heard incessant screams coming from outside, he couldn't ignore it anymore. Now, he stood by the door, watching a boy reel over, crying in pain while another boy stood over him, standing nearly as still as a next-gen terminator.

Alvaro walked closer to them and pointed the wooden spatula he held at them, shouting, "Hey! What the heck is going on out here?"

Mitch was still busy howling and trying to stop his hands from flapping around while Danny watched on, savoring every single moment of it. Without moving the rest of his body, Danny rotated his head, his neck creaking mechanically as he shot Alvaro a fierce look.

The light of a passing car shone on his face at that moment. Seeing his face, Alvaro quickly retracted his steps. "Fuck!" he exclaimed as he lost his footing and fell onto the cold, hard floor. Instantly, he scampered away with his hands until he was back on his feet; then he ran inside the diner as fast as his heavy legs could carry him, locking the door behind him.

As soon as the chef was out of sight, Danny moved closer to Mitch and tapped him on the shoulder. At that moment, Mitch made one of the biggest mistakes of his life—he looked up. Instantly, Danny landed a heavy punch, rattling his teeth as he sucker-punched him, sending him flying into the dumpster. It was quite a sight to behold as midair, his broken hands began to flap about like chicken wings. Mitch landed in the dumpster with great force, making the metal lid close over him.

Danny, however, wasn't done with him yet. He hurried over to the dumpster and flipped open the lid; Mitch's muffled screams grew much louder.

He pulled him onto his feet and placed a hand on his head to hold him steadily in place.

"Help! Help! Fuck you!" Mitch yelled into his face.

Danny slowly wiped the saliva off his face. "Quiet now, boy," he said as he jammed his hand into Mitch's moving mouth. The sounds became muffled as Danny fondled around inside his mouth. Suddenly, he began to retract his hand slowly, and the bone-chilling sound that accompanied it was that of flesh tearing.

Tears rolled down Mitch's face as he shook his head vigorously. However, he was unable to free himself from the vice-like grip on his head. When Danny's hand finally came free of his mouth, lying in his palm was his bloody prize—Mitch's tongue.

The horrified look on Mitch's face was incomprehensible as he stared at his own tongue. His mouth began moving rapidly as in speech, but no words came forth; all he did was cough up and spit out blood.

<hr />

As Keith bent down his head to scoop some cheerios into his mouth, he heard the sound of a siren overshadowing that of the loud country music that was being blasted in the diner. He sat upright and glanced out of the window; after a few seconds, a cop car pulled up in front of the establishment. Had they found out that they were the ones that burned down Danny's house? He quickly pulled out his phone and texted Mitch, asking for his whereabouts. He had said he was only stepping out for a walk, and that had been a while ago. Keith, however, remained seated where he was, quietly wondering what was happening. Outside, Officers Teresa and Doug climbed out of the squad car and began walking toward the diner. Plastered on Teresa's face was a smug smile.

Doug was speaking frantically, "...And I was like, it's not a gun in my pants, I promise... I swear." He chuckled heartily at his own joke.

Teresa cocked her eyebrows and stopped for a minute, looking down at him. "Wow! Really? That's it?" she asked, unmoved by what he had said.

Doug's excitement was hard to contain as he continued, saying, "I know right. I said the same..."

He was interrupted by Debbie as she rushed out of the diner, screaming for help. She ran directly into Teresa's arms and began to sob on her shoulder. Teresa's mouth was slightly ajar as she quickly tried to process what had just occurred.

"Hey! What's wrong?" Doug asked with a sheepish look on his face.

Debbie detached herself from the hug and looked up into Teresa's eyes as she began stammering. "I... I'm so sorry—He—he tried to, he tried to ra-ra-rape me."

Teresa became alert; there was nothing more she hated

than predators who picked on women just because they considered them a weaker sex. "Where?" she asked.

Debbie pointed to the diner with a shaky index finger. "At the back," she said. Instantly, the two police officers began running.

Danny grabbed the hair on Mitch's head tightly as he slapped him across the face several times to jolt him back to reality. "Look at me..." he barked.

Mitch's neck shook groggily as he struggled to maintain focus. Danny pulled him up by the head off of the ground, his arms dangling by his side like sausages. As Danny held him up before him, several pieces of hair began to rip off from his scalp; Danny didn't sympathize with him a bit.

As Mitch stood suspended in the air, Danny placed his hand on the side of his face, turning him slightly to look directly at him. Mitch whimpered and pleaded to be released, but his voice failed him. Slowly, Danny crept his hand up until it was covering Mitch's face and his palm rested on the bridge of his nose. Then he curled four of his fingers forward and began pushing two into each of

Mitch's eyes.

Mitch trembled as a result of intense pain, his heart nearly failing him as he heard the squishing sound of his eyeballs. He began to cough up blood in agony as Danny's fingers continued to pierce deeper and deeper into his skull.

At that moment, Doug and Teresa appeared from behind the corner of the building. "Freeze!" they both yelled.

Danny glanced in their direction, his fingers still lodged in Mitch's head. His hoodie had shifted back slightly. The outfit he wore was the same one he had on when he had visited her earlier; Teresa recognized him instantly.

"Danny?" she called out hesitantly.

Suddenly, Doug fired two shots at Danny, hitting him squarely in the chest. "Hold your fire! You dumb fuck!" Teresa shouted.

Luckily for Danny, he was unharmed as the bullets had no effect on him. He shot a dangerous stare at Doug, making the officer tremble in his boots.

Meanwhile, Mitch still whimpered where he was hanging. Danny placed his mouth to his ear. "I'll be back," he whispered in the softest tone he could muster. Then he detached his fingers from his eye sockets and slowly put

Mitch down on the ground.

He threw the hair that came undone from Mitch's scalp down beside him where he laid curled up, whimpering like a dog run over by a truck. Slowly, he turned back to face the cops, flicking the sticky bits of Mitch's eyes off of his finger. He looked up at Teresa as his hoodie finally slipped away, revealing his full face for the first time. "You look good," he said.

Seeing his darkened face, Doug's mouth went aghast as he recoiled in fear. His gun quickly went up again as he used all his willpower to stop himself from shooting.

Meanwhile, Teresa eyed Danny with concern as she took in all his facial features, the veins running all over his face, down his neck and disappearing under his sweater, undoubtedly, to continue the network of darkened blood vessels. "What happened to you?" she asked.

Danny shrugged as he wiped the remaining goo on his finger against his cloth. "I became me!" he simply stated.

Teresa shook her head in disapproval. "No, this isn't you... You need help, Danny..." she said softly.

Doug, however, didn't exhibit her calmness. "Turn around and put your hands behind your head. Now!" he said in a squeaky voice, his gun still trained on his target.

Slowly, Danny put up his hands in surrender and

turned his back to the cops. He tilted his ears slightly as if he was listening to a sound from afar; then a mischievous smile appeared on his face.

A few seconds later, the back door of the diner flung open and out rushed Keith. Startled by the unexpected movement, Doug pointed to the intruder and shot at Keith's feet.

"Jeez. What the fuck, man?" Keith yelled, jumping back just in time to miss catching a bullet in his leg.

"Shit," Doug blurted. His hands began to tremble as he realized he could have made a grave mistake that would've derailed his life.

"Put that gun away now!" Teresa said.

Doug quickly placed the gun back in its holster. As he regained his composure, he began looking around as he shouted, "Where did he go?"

Teresa quickly glanced at where Danny had stood moments earlier. In his place, she saw nothing but thin air. He must've escaped while they were distracted, she thought. She heard a loud scurrying noise coming from the forest at the other side of the road and she knew Danny was long gone.

Keith looked stunned as he saw his friend writhing

and moaning on the ground. "What the hell happened here?" he asked as he saw the trail of blood around Mitch. He quickly ran to his side.

The two cops ignored his question as they began walking toward them. "We need to get him to the hospital, ASAP. Doug, call an ambulance," Teresa ordered.

The tinted light coming from the cellphone glowed against Mrs. Hork's eyes where she sat behind her office desk. She hadn't planned to stay this long in school but there was some pressing business she needed to address that day and had unexpectedly drawn out into the night.

"Okay. Just... get back to me as soon as you can, the entire staff is awaiting your response... Alright, thank you... bye," she said to the person at the other end of the call.

"Phew," she sighed as she hung up the call and began rubbing her forehead. She was stressed out more than ever. The desk lamp on the table before her shone light on her weary face.

Mrs. Hork let out a long sigh as she continued to rub her forehead in an attempt to de- stress. "Time for me to leave now, I guess," she muttered to her words. Her voice, even though just above a whisper, carried far across the empty hallways outside the staff room.

Mrs. Hork straightened her blouse before she took off her glasses. Taking a small handkerchief out of her desk drawer, she began to wipe the lenses with it. As she raised her head slightly, she noticed a blurred figure standing by a corner close to the door. "Jeff, is that you?" she called out to no response.

She began to get uneasy as she knew that Jeff, the old janitor, she was supposed to be alone in the school at that time of the night. She quickly wore her glasses again only to realize that what she had been scared of was nothing but a coat.

She chuckled nervously. "Haha, that was close," she said to herself, her hand on her chest as if she could calm her thumping heartbeat with the touch.

From where she sat, she began putting away the files on her table into the appropriate desk drawers. She put the books away as well, tucking them neatly into the various compartments her desk possessed.

Then she picked up a framed picture from the table and stared at it for a moment. The image in the photo was that of her younger self giving a valedictorian speech in front of a large group of people. "How the time flies," she muttered. A smile crossed her face as she recollected her fondest memory—her high school graduation. Indeed, she had peaked in high school, Mrs. Hork admitted to herself.

Aubrey Hork was the brightest student in her high school, and she had graduated top of her class, with the world at her feet. However, life had taken an unexpected turn down the road, and now here she was, stuck with teaching a bunch of cocky, dumb, unappreciative high schoolers.

Mrs. Hork's facial expression slowly changed from a smile to a scowl as she mused on how much she hated her job. What she detested most about teaching was the kids she had to smile and put up with, many of whom didn't even want to be in school. She silently lamented about her pay, which was hardly enough to cater for her expenses. This was partly why she often took her frustration out on her students, she thought.

Mrs. Hork stared at a different photo, revealing Elinore and her from at least a decade ago, wondering where all the years had gone. She focused on her bright smile in the picture, tracing her finger on Elinore's face. "I miss you," she said to herself.

"I miss her too," a familiar voice said from behind.

Reflecting in the glass frame of the photo was a figure standing directly behind her, and this time Aubrey knew it wasn't a coat hanger.

She began to hear a low, guttural grunt like the sound of boar breathing.

Mrs. Hork rose slowly, and a pair of hands quickly shot out and grabbed her by the shoulders. Before she could react, a great force pushed her down, slamming her back into the seat.

7

F

From behind her, she heard a young male voice say, "You... You've made my life a living hell... F... F..." She knew the voice to be Danny, and when Danny stepped forward and stood beside her, recognition dawned on her face.

Danny began to jolt her chair forward, making her close to slamming her face against the table before pulling her back. He repeated this a few times, making the woman shiver and tremble, scared.

"F. F! F! F!" he repeated in a deep, surreal, metallic voice each time he pushed her forward.

Then, it all stopped in a moment. Aubrey Hork trembled where she sat, the sudden silence filled her with dread as she anticipated what was to come next. "Uhhh. Uhhhh!" she muttered as her body shook vigorously.

Danny took his time, wanting to build up the tension in the woman's heart; he smirked devilishly. As the woman's heavy breathing began to get slower, more stable, Danny suddenly whirled her chair around and roared in her face. The noise was so loud it sounded like a dozen trumpets being blown at once. His cheeks rippled, and the noise grew louder as his mouth seemed to expand like a sinkhole, inviting his target to take a head dive in.

Hot air blew on Mrs. Hork's face, slightly making her hair flail behind her. She had a close view of the channel of dark veins on his face, and coupled with his sickening roar, she chuckled hysterically. Then he began to roar louder, his mouth freakishly extended much wider than earlier.

Mrs. Hork began to scream out loud in fear. Her cries mixed with the incessant terrifying roar created a cacophony that could send chills down the spine of anyone who heard it.

Unfortunately for Jeff, he was close enough to hear the demonic noise echoing through the halls of the school. He was making a cleaning run at that moment, and he was mopping the empty hallway when the screams and cries began. He could sense that the noise was coming from somewhere inside the building but he couldn't tell where exactly. Jeff considered investigating where the noise originated from but his gumption wasn't on board with that plan. It was probably some of the students trying to lure him out and prank him again, he told himself.

Jeff continued mopping the floor, whistling along. Suddenly, the voice crying turned into quick, terrified gasps; Jeff shuffled back upon hearing this. He could make out that it was a feminine voice and after listening for a few seconds longer, he admitted to himself that the fear carried in the cries was too genuine to be a prank.

"Oh, puck it!" he said, a large amount of air escaping through his near-toothless mouth as he spoke.

With that, Jeff picked up his mop bucket and began moving toward the end of the hallway where the noise seemed to be coming from. He walked as fast as his frail legs would allow him, dragging his feet behind him. All along, he was muttering furiously.

Meanwhile, Mrs. Hork's face was beginning to turn white under the assault of the screams. She knew she couldn't take it for much longer before she crashed and fell to the ground.

Danny noticed the change in her eyes as she began to gasp louder. *It would be no fun to scare the woman to death now, would it?* he said to himself. As suddenly as it began,

Danny stopped roaring and closed his mouth. He smiled at the petrified woman and tapped her cheek a few times before he took a few steps back, waiting for her to regain her strength, then he'd move to the second phase of his plans for her. He thought to himself, *is this too much?* The rage inside Danny was complete fire, almost as if Ida and him were sharing rage, driving him to complete judgement for everyone who wronged him.

Aubrey Hork said a silent prayer of thanks as her attacker stopped screaming. She scooped long drags of oxygen into her lungs. Her hands went to the arms of the chair and she gripped it tightly, steadying herself. She looked up at Danny and saw his soulless, black eyes trained on her, watching her every movement. At that moment, her bones chilled as she came to a grave realization—he wasn't done with her yet. Aubrey quickly adjusted her glasses and swallowed hard as she wondered if he was even planning to let her go. As she looked at him again, his staunch composure and clenched cheeks, she knew the odds weren't in her favor.

Suddenly, she sprang up and began running for the door. As she made it halfway, through, she hit a thigh against a chair and nearly tripped. However, she struggled to maintain her balance as she knew if she fell, it was over for her. She glanced back for a second and was surprised to see that Danny was still standing where he was. He wasn't chasing after her, only his eyes followed her. Aubrey was astounded. *What freakish game is this boy playing with me?* she asked herself. However, she didn't want to wait around to find out the answer.

As she made it through the door, she stuck her head out and looked both ways. Spotting the janitor peering into a room a distance away, she shouted at him, "Help me! Please!" Before she spoke, she hadn't intended to burst into tears, however, as she cried out loud, it gave a certain urgency to her plea.

On hearing her cries, Jeff instantly whirled around and spotted the woman close ahead. With his mop bucket in hand, he began to gallop toward her like a horse with a stone in its hoof. "What's ampuning?" he called out.

Mrs. Hork was too scared to say anything else other than crying out for help. The old man didn't look like much of a hero but with his presence and being a potential witness, Aubrey silently prayed that Danny would be deterred from coming after her again.

Jeff saw the woman's legs move as she attempted to run toward him, with her arms wide open as if to embrace him. Jeff increased the pace of his hops. However, as the woman got halfway to meeting him, Danny shot out his hands, wrapping around her waist and pulled her back into the room she had run out from. Instantly, Jeff jumped backward as fear gripped him at what he had just witnessed. He wondered if it wasn't his mind playing tricks on him. Was he beginning to lose his old mind?

"Helllllppp! Don't let him take me!" Mrs. Hork shouted just before she got dragged into the dark abyss of her office where a sinister entity laid patiently in wait for her.

Suddenly, the woman's screams became muffled and moments later, it died down completely. Jeff stood where he was, waiting for a few seconds with the hopes that she would reemerge. However, as the seconds rolled over another, the utter silence was beginning to agitate the old janitor. Summoning up all the courage his frail heart could muster, he began to take cautious steps forward. "Are you okay, ma'am?" he called out in a shaky voice. His breath quickened as he got closer to the staff office. There was still no sound coming from the room; all Jeff could see was a soft glow reflecting faintly on the hallway floor.

"Minsus Honk? Are you there?" he said again, to no response. The tension he was feeling had multiplied exponentially by then. The logical part of him suggested that he turn around and go call for help. However, his inquisitive spirit got the best of him. Besides, whatever attacked the woman could come after him if he tried to go all the way to get a phone from the janitor's office, which was located at the other side of the building. He couldn't win a race against toddlers, lest a supernatural monster, he admitted to himself.

As the tug of war raged on in his scantily haired head, his feet kept on moving forward. Suddenly, a head shot out through the door, making Jeff stop dead in his tracks. Although the suddenness of the person's movement was scary, what baffled Jeff the most was that it wasn't Mrs. Hork's head; it was a young man's.

The person was completely clad in black. In the dull ambience of the place, he looked like a ninja from a low-budget movie. Spotting the old janitor, his eyes locked on him instantly.

"Danny...?" Jeff mumbled as recognition dawned on him. The look of confusion on the old man's face was priceless as his jaw dropped.

Before he could get an answer from the boy who used to work with him, Danny disappeared back into the room and shut the door behind him with a loud bang, shaking it at its hinges.

For five seconds, everything went still. All Jeff could hear was his own heavy breathing. As he began to hope it was all over, a shrill cry pierced the air and it quickly turned into bloodcurdling screams.

Jeff ran and tripped over the mop bucket. The soapy water spilled and drenched him before splattering all over the hallway floor. In the face of fear, Jeff didn't seem to care much about his wet clothes as he began crawling on all fours away from the staff office. As soon as he was able to get his grip, he scampered onto his shaky feet and began galloping toward his office.

***

The expression on the orderly's face as he pushed the wheelchair down the hospital hallway was that of pure boredom. The young orderly, with curly brown hair and a smirk plastered at the corner of his mouth moved nearly as still as the boy who sat in the leather seat that was fitted into the wheelchair. Every person who passed by them or saw them had an incomprehensible look of shock on their faces. Many tried to act polite by only taking occasional glances at them. However, some people didn't display that much discretion as they gawked at the boy openly with looks of shock and disgust on their faces. "Oh, wow!" a man who had come for his chemotherapy session had said aloud.

The orderly didn't pay any of the onlookers much attention; their looks of pity or disgust at the body he was ferrying had no emotional effect on him; it didn't move him an inch. He was working a lot of hours for meager pay. Besides, he was the one stuck with rolling around the mummy-like figure in the wheelchair, not them. The thought that dominated his mind was for his shift to end on time so he could go home to resume his *Call Of Duty* battle, the game being one of the few reasons for his existence.

The wheels made a soft screeching noise, gliding over the shiny tiled floor as he made a sharp turn into a room to the left.

"Wow!" Teresa exclaimed, taken aback by the sight before her. Mitch was bandaged from the top of his head down the length of his entire torso. A clinic patient's robe was worn over the bandages. His arms were placed in casts, with his left wrist handcuffed to the arm of the wheelchair. Teresa had ordered an officer to do that as a preventive measure—after all, Mitch was still under arrest for attempted rape. Although, with the way he looked now, Teresa was fairly certain that he probably would remain a celibate for the rest of his life.

Standing beside Teresa in the hospital room was the doctor in charge of Mitch's treatment as well as a few nurses. Many of the latter weren't really assigned to the patient but they had come to see the badly-wounded casualty of karma whose rumors were already making rounds around town.

As the orderly wheeled the patient into the room, the nurses looked aghast and they began to chatter amongst themselves in low voices.

"This is just... Frankly, I've never seen anything like this before," Doctor Evans said. He stood aside to give the orderly some space to pass.

"I know. Poor kid," Teresa replied as she and the nurses followed the doctor's movements and took a few steps back themselves.

The orderly pushed the wheelchair until it reached the side of the bed. Then, he turned it around to face the people in the room. He gave the doctor a curt nod before walking briskly out of the room.

Doctor Evans squinted his eyes in an attempt to observe him from where he stood. After a few seconds of silence, his eyes widened back to their normal positions. He stood erect, flexing his shoulders slightly as he shook his head. "The damage is extensive, and there is nothing anyone can do about it. It's sad he will never have a normal life again."

"Really?" Teresa asked, a hint of intrigue in her voice rather than pity. In truth, she felt no remorse for the boy who had sexually assaulted a girl and may have harmed her even more if someone hadn't intervened.

Meanwhile, hearing the professional's verdict on his health status, Mitch began to shake in the wheelchair. He began to mumble behind the bandages.

"Easy now, boy, you don't want to cause yourself more harm," Dr. Evans said. The nurses rushed over to Mitch's side to dispatch an injection to calm him.

"I see you have a lot to handle," Teresa said, pointing to the boy in the wheelchair who was struggling to prevent the nurses from injecting him, waving his blind head around. "Kindly give me periodic updates on his status."

"Sure, I'll do the needful and send you reports... Have a nice day, officer," the doctor said.

"Great. You too."

With that, Teresa turned around and began walking out of the hospital room, wondering what Mitch had done to Danny to deserve this from the relatively harmless young man she had known.

As she stepped out of the room and turned the corner, she saw Doug standing in the hallway waiting for her, with his arms at his back and his head slightly bent like a billionaire's butler.

Spotting her, he began to take hurried steps toward her, meeting her halfway. "Can we talk about what just happened back at the diner," Doug said in a low voice which couldn't disguise the hint of excitement in it.

"No, wait till I get back," Teresa retorted as he walked down the remaining length of the hallway. She pulled in the glass double doors and stepped out of the hospital.

Keith tapped his foot on the dusty floor a couple times in rapid succession. He was beginning to grow uneasy where he rested against his truck. He looked up at the front door of Jessica's house, and he began to wonder when she was going to come out. He had appeared without calling her, hoping to catch her before she went to school. As he waited by his truck parked outside, he could hear the sound of her voice coming from inside the house.

He hadn't waited much longer before the front door opened and Jessica stepped out onto the porch. Keith was surprised to see Mikayla behind her.

As soon as Jessica saw Keith standing outside her home, she rolled her eyes and crossed her arms in front of her chest, with the small pile of books in her hands pressing against her breasts. Seeing her defiant act, Keith beckoned for her to come over.

After considering it for a few seconds, Jessica began walking toward the truck, with Mikayla following closely behind her like a Labrador.

"What do you want?" Jessica asked as she stood in front of her. Keith was a good foot taller than her, and she had to lift her head up in order to look into his eyes.

"Get in the car. We'll talk on the road," he responded. He began walking toward the driver's side.

"Where's Mitch?" Mikayla asked as she glanced into truck and saw it was empty.

Keith stopped in his tracks and glanced back at Mikky. A pitiful look crossed his face and he nodded slightly at her before opening the car door and sitting behind the wheel.

Mikayla was confused and scared. She knew how insep-
arable the two boys were, and if Mitch wasn't here, then
something must have befallen him. The look of compassion Keith had given her said it all. A chill ran down her
spine as she climbed into the backseat of the car.

Keith turned on the ignition and pulled onto the road
slowly as he began driving the car occupied by three petrified souls to school.

———

The huge tires of the truck make a loud screeching
noise as it pulled up into the parking lot of the school.
The students' space was located at the front of the school
providing quick access to the main entrance.

Keith parked between two saloon cars, making the
truck seem like a giant. "Aren't we late?" Jessica asked.

"Yeah, twenty minutes late," Mikayla responded,
glancing at her watch.

"I guess everybody woke up late today," Jessica said,
as she looked around. The whole parking lot up to the
doors of the school was crowded. Students walked around
casually and chatted excitedly in little groups. As Jessica
observed on, she noticed none of the students acted like
they had classes to attend. She became intrigued.

Meanwhile, Keith jumped down from the truck and slammed the door behind him. He pulled his letterman jacket closely around him and kept his head low as he waited for the girls to come out of the truck. He looked around and instantly recognized that this scenario he had seen it many times before—a very juicy gossip was spreading through the school. His stomach turned as he wondered if the milling students were talking about Mitch. Keith quickly shook the thought out of his head as an image of his friend's contorted and mangled body came to mind.

"C'mon, girls, let's move," he said, anger beginning to well up inside him.

"Calm your fucking tits," Jessica retorted in spite as she climbed out of the truck.

Mikayla was already on the ground, her eyes darting around suspiciously as if a shadow was going to snatch her in the daylight. Without waiting for the others, she began to head toward the school building.

Jessica didn't make any attempt to recall her. Instead, she walked around the truck to stand before Keith, shooting him a skull piercing glare.

Keith cowered. "Look. I'm sorry about all this. I never meant for it to—"

Suddenly, a scream pierced the air and everybody stopped what they were doing instantly as they looked in the direction where the noise had come from.

A girl was standing at the side of the school building, screaming at the top of her lungs.

Many of the students quickly rushed to see what all the fuss was about. However, as they arrived at the scene, the look of excitement on their faces quickly turned to awe and disgust. The scream was picked up by several of the new arrivals and it soon began sounding like a choir of wailers. However, the people around paid little attention to the bickering as their eyes were set on something bigger, which couldn't be seen by those standing at the front of the school.

"What the hell is happening over there?" Keith asked rhetorically as he read the look of dread on the faces of the onlookers.

Jessica was puzzled by the commotion as well, and she began to move toward the place. "Hey, wait up!" Keith called out.

Jessica ignored him completely as she navigated through the herd of students who had begun teeming in the direction she was going. Finally, she got clear and stood face to face with the source of the commotion.

Her jaw dropped as she stared ahead at the incomprehensible sight.

A light pole at the back of the building had an unusual object attached to it; Jessica's teacher, Mrs. Hork. At the top of the metal pole, the woman was tied tightly and held in place by barbed wire. Blood was dripping from all over her body where the crooked wire tore into her flesh. The woman was completely naked, and deep gashes were visible on her body as the barbed wire was wrapped tautly around her chest and down to her knees, leaving her legs dangling. Crimson red blood flowed down the course of the spiral wire.

To the utmost surprise of Jessica, somehow, the woman was still alive.

Mrs. Hork had her eyes turned to the sky while she mumbled. From where Jessica stood, she couldn't make out the words the woman was uttering. Just then, the teacher looked down at crowd before her and began laughing hysterically.

The students shuffled back in horror, and many of them ran away. Jessica, however, stood her ground. She studied the woman carefully.

At that moment, Keith broke through the crowd and nearly jumped out at the sight of the suspended woman on the pole. "What the fuck."

As he appeared, the woman's eyes suddenly turned to the pair.

"Oh my God!" Jessica exclaimed as she noticed something freakishly new about the woman's appearance. Mrs. Hork's eyes had turned a light gray shade and the white part of her eyeballs had completely disappeared.

"Danny…" Keith stated in a hushed tone as he recalled where he had seen the soulless stare before.

Jessica glanced sideways at him and a silent message passed between them. Without saying a word to each other, Jessica and Keith turned around to leave the crowd.

Unbeknownst to them, Mrs. Hork's eyes fixated on them, and her hysterical cackle grew louder.

The steam from the coffee in Teresa's hand spiraled above and turned into warm vapor as she stared at her desk, oblivious of the chemical reaction resulting from the beverage she was calming her nerves with. A look of puzzlement was visible on her face as she tapped her foot against the floor in anxiety.

Just then, the door flung open and in stepped Doug. On sighting him, Teresa adjusted her stance and wiped the worried look off her face. She placed the coffee cup on the desk and turned to face him. "I told you to wait," she said in irritation.

"Something tells me he isn't going anywhere," Doug responded, ignoring her comment. He went over to the chair at his side of the desk and sat down. Without waiting for her response, he continued, "Our suspect's name is Danny." He tossed a file on the desk recklessly as he continued giving his oral report. "His house was burnt down and a body was found inside. We have reasons to believe it's his father, David, who I've come to learn is a sort of legend around here."

Teresa rolled her eyes at his last comment. "Go on," she said.

Doug threw his hands up in the air. "That's all we have for now. The boy is nowhere to be found."

Teresa pondered his words and nodded. "Our main priority is the students. Call Principal Red, no more stu—"

"And say what exactly?" Doug retorted.

"That the school is no longer a safe place for students and staff. Something needs to be done soon."

At that, Doug jumped to his feet. Losing his boyish demeanor, he began to take quick steps toward her. "He took two shots... Son of a bitch didn't even flinch!" he exclaimed, bewildered. "I think we should call in the big guns."

Teresa looked down as thoughts raced through her head. She hadn't wanted it to get to this, but deep down, she knew a confrontation was unavoidable at this point. Whatever had provoked Danny, he had taken it too far, and he needed to be put in check.

Teresa heaved a long sigh. "Call it in."

Doug's sheepish smile appeared on his face once again. With the help coming, maybe they would have a chance against the monster, he thought. Hope filled his mind with warmth.

8

CATCH AND RELEASE

Danny was beginning to find a home in the serene atmosphere of the forest. Many people would call Witch's Creek a creepy place—heck, he had even thought so before. However, seeing with his own eyes now, the huge forest was nothing but peaceful. Trouble only came to those who sought it. And sought, Gill and his friends had.

Gill had paid for his sins with his life, and Danny had given him a merciless befitting sendoff.

Now, Danny lay on the forest floor once again, surrounded by trees. Thick vines the size of a human's arm wrapped around him, but he felt no discomfort. Rather, he was exhilarated by the memories of the act of vengeance.

The memory of Mrs. Hork's titties jiggling while he dragged her down the school hallway on his way to tying her to the light pole was still fresh in his head. It wasn't sexual gratification he was feeling, rather, he truly enjoyed every discomfort he caused his enemies.

Two down... Well, and a very deformed half, he thought. Danny felt a little annoyed by the interruption of Teresa and her cop buddy before he could finish dealing with Mitch. He had a few other things in mind for the bastard, and he hated that his hard work had now become half completed.

He had to wait and wait. But now, the delay was over.

Danny's eyes shot open, the white in his eyeballs appearing briefly before his black pupils dilated and kept growing wide until it covered the whole space in his eyes.

He sprang onto his feet and began heading out of the forest in the town's direction.

———

Wentworth Hospital was unusually lousy at that time of the day. A middle aged woman had brought her four-years-old triplets for dentals, and the little kids were crying in the lobby, even before they were called into the doctor's room.

Meanwhile, at another wing at the other side of the building, Nurse Cindy was rolling a cart into a room in the intensive care unit. Her blonde hair was tied in a bun at the back of her head. She had a cheerful air about her and even the sight of the badly bandaged patient before her couldn't dampen her bright smile.

Cindy looked over at Mitch in the wheelchair he sat handcuffed to its arm.

"Thought I'd stop by and see how you were doing," she said, smiling politely even though the patient couldn't see her.

Mitch became uneasy, and he began to make inaudible noises beneath the bandages. His body began shaking and he bumped his cuffs violently.

"Okay, easy, easy... How about some breakfast?" Cindy said in an attempt to pacify him. She rolled over the small cart with a cup of orange juice on it and set it in front of him. The cup had a red straw in it, the size of the thin slit cut into the bandage on Mitch's mouth.

"Here, I'll help you," Cindy said as she lifted the cup with one hand while she guided the straw to his mouth with the other. "Okay... just lean forward a little... I have some orange juice..."

Suddenly, another nurse popped her head in. "Cindy, guess who has a girlfriend!" she said in a hushed tone accustomed to gossiping.

Startled, Cindy whirled around quickly and spilled the juice on Mitch, unknowingly. "No... Don't tell me!" she exclaimed, irritated.

The other nurse chirped on excitedly, "Come look at his Instagram!"

At that moment, Cindy picked up on the cue and her eyes grew wider. Instantly, she dropped the cup on the cart, spilling some more of the colored juice on Mitch's body. Without a single glance at him, she hurried out of the room.

In protest, Mitch began to mumble louder and shake angrily in his chair, but no one paid him any attention. *These fucking whores are messing with me*, he said in his head, no place to vent his anger. *Curse you, Danny*, he said silently, thinking of ways he would exert his revenge on him when he got out of the hospital. As cynical ideas floated in his head, a smile appeared on Mitch's face for the first time since the accident.

***

Danny pulled the hoodie over his face tighter as he stood at the entrance of Wentworth Hospital. He wasn't attempting to hide his face since if there was somewhere a person with a deformed face like his should be, it should be at a hospital. He was right at home. The reason Danny was maintaining his cover was because he was trying to avoid being recognized and his plan being foiled once again. He knew there were surveillance cameras all over the floor, and he had come prepared with a distraction plan.

He placed his hand holding a bottle inside his jacket as he pushed the double doors in and entered. He had sprayed a fair amount of perfume on himself so as to cover up the smell of the content of the bottle—gasoline. He began walking down the hallway, strutting casually so as to eradicate any suspicions.

At the reception to his right where all the surveillance monitors were, he saw a group of nurses huddled around their colleague holding a mobile phone. All their eyes were focused on the phone's screen.

Danny shook his head, wondering what they were all excited about. One particular blonde amongst the nurses was chuckling heartily. "She's so ugly!" she exclaimed.

Danny realized that they were fully engrossed in what they were watching and he didn't need to use his distraction tactic anymore. He took the opportunity and began walking down the hall toward the intensive care unit.

He peered into each of the rooms at both sides of the hall and when his eyes set on his target in a room to the left, he smiled and entered.

"Morning, Mitch," he said in a sing song tone as he closed the door behind him.

Instantly, Mitch sat upright. He began to murmur in fear. Shaking his head vigorously, he began to jerk backward in his seat, thereby pushing the wheelchair until it slammed into the wall behind him, the metals making loud screeching and creaking noises.

Danny took a few steps forward, making his footsteps loud enough for Mitch to hear and taking each one slowly so as to prolong his dread. "I bet you never expected this..." Danny said, crouching before him so that they were at face level with each other.

Mitch was scared out of his mind. He began to rattle his cuffs louder with the hope of getting someone's attention. However, nobody heard nor came to his aid.

At that moment, Danny pulled the bottle out of his jacket and held it in front of Mitch. "Smell that?" he asked, jolting the bottle a little to make the smell rise.

Mitch screamed as much as he could but the only sound that got out through the wrapper around his head was a muffled noise. He tried to stand but he was held in place by the handcuffs. As he made violent jerking motions, blood began to seep into the bandages, tainting them with red as the stitches on his face ripped.

"You left this behind," Danny said as he brandished a switch blade in his hand.

Mitch's ears cocked as he heard the familiar sound of his blade. He began to push the wheelchair harder backward but it was held in place staunchly by the wall.

Danny brought the handle of the knife closely to Mitch's open palm. As soon as the latter tried to grab it, Danny quickly took it out of his reach. He flipped the knife around and stabbed Mitch's bandaged hand, hooking it down against the leather arm of the wheelchair.

Mitch screamed in pain but to Danny, it sounded like a forced whimper. He stood up and emptied the content of the bottle on Mitch, drenching him with the flammable liquid.

"Don't worry," Danny said. Leaning closer until he could hear Mitch's rapid breathing, he added in a whisper, "No one's gonna miss you."

Sowing the final seed of fear in his soul, Danny placed his hand between the short distance between them. Suddenly, he snapped his fingers and a sparkle erupted, catching on the gasoline, and it engulfed both of them.

—— ❦ ——

Cindy was the first to notice the smoke drifting into the hallway just across the room she had just left not too long ago. "Guys, come and see this," she called out, pointing to the monitor screen.

The other nurses were still preoccupied with their gossip. One of them looked back at what Cindy was saying and yelled, "Oh my gosh! Smoke!"

The remaining nurses instantly turned around and began to scream, panicking. "Fire!" another shouted.

Cindy lost her senses and she began to run toward the intensive care unit, ignoring the calls of her colleagues to stop. As she arrived at the scene, to her utmost horror, she realized that the smoke was coming from the room she was assigned to.

Cindy watched on as the patient squirmed in his wheelchair while the fire caught the bandages all over his body. She grabbed a fire extinguisher from the wall and tried to approach the room, but she retreated as the fire was already raging hard and the entrance had been covered in flames. At that moment, she noticed that the patient wasn't the only person in the room. The second person was also on fire but he didn't display any agony.

Cindy was shocked by this discovery. She blinked twice to be sure she wasn't hallucinating, and yet, the other figure was still in the room. At that moment, the person turned around slowly to face her.

While doused in flames, the person smiled at her. Cindy's heart dropped and she ran back the way she had come, screaming at the top of her lungs as her arms flailed frantically above her head.

⁓

The cloudy sky was a little dark even though the sun was just rising to its peak. Keith paid little attention to the weather as he sat parked in front of Jessica's house for the second time that day. He tapped the wheels in agitation as he waited. Close to the peak of his patience, he began to push the horn button. The truck let out deep, honking sounds in quick succession.

"C'mon... Come on..." he muttered. He heard a shuffling noise coming from the woods behind him and he stared at the forest, dreading the emergence of Danny. His paranoia increased as the noise came to an abrupt halt.

At that moment, the front door to Jessica's house opened and she stepped out.

At the sound of the door opening, Keith quickly looked at the direction and was disappointed that once again, she wasn't alone; her father stood beside her on the porch.

In a slow motion, she shook her head and Keith got the drift immediately; she wasn't allowed to come with him. "Fuck this!" he said as he kicked the gear into action and drove onto the main road before flooring the gas and disappearing down the winding road ahead.

He turned on the car radio and began to play John Denver's "Country Road, Take Me Home." He figured if he was going to die soon, he should go out in style. Keith began to hum and as it got to the chorus, he began yelling, "West Virginia, mountain mama... Take me home, country road..." He pumped his fist up while his second hand banged against the steering wheel in gyration. Other people driving by watched his solo performance in his truck, many of them wondering what strain of marijuana the young man was high on.

Keith paid none of them any attention as he continued vibing to the music coming from the CD player. However, he hadn't gotten too far that he noticed the "low fuel" light blinking.

Luckily for him, there was a gas station not too far ahead. Upon arriving, he exited the truck. He stood for a second to look around, something that had become sort of an impulsive ritual for him ever since the attack on Mitch at the diner. He dreaded Danny sneaking up on him. If he was to die, he wanted to face his death head on.

After ensuring his perpetual safety, he entered the mart at the gas station.

Inside, the clerk was fixated on the small LCD television before him. As he saw Keith enter, he gave him a cursory glance before turning back to the game show he was watching.

Keith was appalled by the man's negligence and he decided to capitalize on it. He headed down the aisle and entered the grocery section. After glancing around to be sure that the clerk wasn't looking, he grabbed a pack of beef jerky and hid it in the back pocket of his jeans. He moved on to the confectionery section and seeing a mini section for chocolates and candies, he grabbed a handful of candy bars and stuffed it beneath his shirt.

Keith quickly turned around and walked briskly out of the mart. Without glancing back, he walked straight to the truck and emptied his stolen wares in the backseat.

Then he climbed out and went to the fuel pump to fill up his gas tank.

He shifted with uneasiness as he held the nozzle to the fuel tank. Turning around slowly, he noticed the clerk was no longer watching the television, instead, his eyes were trained on him, eyeing him suspiciously.

Without filling up his tank to the point he had planned, he returned the nozzle to the pump and jumped back into his truck before zooming off.

***

"You think he's going to kill us?" Mikayla asked, voicing the question that weighed on her mind.

"I don't know. Better question is, do we deserve it?" Jessica replied. She had been considering it for a while now, whether Danny would try to kill her as well. She knew he had attempted to take Mikayla's life once, and Jessica wondered if he would pardon her for being his friend. "That's not the Danny I knew. The old one couldn't hurt a fly... But he's gone... We have to look out for ourselves now," she stated emotionlessly.

She and Mikayla lay side by side on the bed, staring at the ceiling. It was late in the evening and the main source of illumination in the room was a fluorescent bulb, which washed the space over with white light.

Jessica crossed her legs and had her palms placed behind her head, with her elbows at acute angles.

The two girls were lounging calmly as if they had no care in the world. They didn't know what the future held for them, but at that moment, all they wanted to do was enjoy the comforting presence of each other.

Suddenly, Jessica jumped up, startling Mikayla with her unexpected movement. Seeing the look of confusion on her friend's face, Jessica began to laugh. "Relax..." she said as she walked over to her drawer. She shifted the whole structure forward and reached into the crevice behind it, pulling out a bottle of whiskey.

Jessica returned the drawer to its normal position and turned around to face her friend with a wide grin.

Spotting the half-full bottle of alcohol, Mikayla smiled.

Jessica produced two glasses from a small compartment in her wardrobe. "Let's blow off some steam."

"Hell yeah!" Mikayla responded, enjoying the sweet taste of rebellion.

Teresa turned on her desk lamp as she couldn't strain her eyes to read with the little ray of light coming into the room. She flipped through the pile of papers and files on her desk, observing the content carefully, all of which pertained to Danny. In such a small town, she wondered why it was so difficult to find a disfigured young man with no friends, no connections, and nowhere to hide.

The biggest question on the officer's mind was what his motive was for committing those gruesome murders. His mode of operation and choice of victims made her deduce that it was an act of retribution. However, what exactly had caused him to go on a rampage? The answer eluded her, and as she thought harder, she felt a migraine forming.

Teresa placed her palm against her forehead.

Just then, the door opened and Doug walked in, nodding at her.

"Oh, not again..." Teresa lamented as she sensed the officer was about to drop some bad news on her lap.

"Oh yeah! Not good," Doug replied, validating her fears.

Teresa sighed heavily. She reached into her drawer and pulled out a bottle of aspirin. She popped two tablets into her mouth before she got up and told her fellow officer to lead the way. *It's going to be a long night,* she thought as she closed her office door behind her.

Little did she know how true her notion would be.

~~~

Keith stretched out his hand and grabbed the rear view mirror, adjusting it slightly to the right. After being satisfied that he could clearly see any vehicle that might approach, he reached down and pushed the next button on the CD Player. After a few seconds of delay, *Ring of Fire* by Johnny Cash rang through the truck.

Keith bobbed his head along to the rhythm of the rock song.

The sun had nearly disappeared from the sky, so he turned on his headlights and he sped down the deserted road.

As he loudly chanted the lyrics of the song, he took his eyes off the road for a split second since he was sure he was the only person ferrying the path at that moment.

Suddenly, his headlights caught a deer standing in the middle of the road. Keith was oblivious as he was preoccupied in his attempt to pick up a beer from the bag on the passenger's seat.

After shuffling for a few seconds, he picked up the can of beer and looked up a little too late to see the deer a yard away.

Moving at high speed, he made a grave mistake of slamming the brake. The truck veered off the road and tipped over, turning upside down in a shallow ditch by the roadside. The horn kept sounding as the wiring got damaged.

Meanwhile, the deer stared at the upturned truck. Then it hopped off the road and into the forest, its mission completed.

At the ditch, the door to the driver's side of the truck opened with a loud creak as the already bent metal became contorted even more. Keith had suffered a concussion and he was close to losing consciousness. However, his brain registered a hand wrapping around his leg and pulling him out of the truck. He didn't feel any pain as his body slammed against the ground with a loud thud.

His head hit a stone and he blacked out.

Unbeknownst to him, the darkened hand was dragging him to Witch's Creek, where it all began.

9

GOOD BOY

I'm in deep shit! was the first thought that came to Keith's mind when he awoke. A gash was on his forehead and blood was slowly dripping down onto his neck.

His head lolled from side to side as he tried to regain his consciousness. He attempted to touch and feel the wound on his head, but to his utmost horror, he realized he had been tied to a tree.

Instantly, he jolted back to life as he looked around. Unsurprisingly, he found that he was in a dark forest with obnoxiously tall, straight trees. *Witch's Creek, no doubt,* he thought. It was night time already as he noticed that the moon and the stars were out.

He heard footsteps approaching him from behind. He tried to crane his head to see who it was but he couldn't see past the tree until the person walked up to stand before him and tossed Mitch's switch blade in his lap.

Keith had guessed that it would be Danny and his assumption was correct. However, all the fears he had tried to bury began to surface again as he came to the obvious conclusion that he was out of his depth and deep in enemy territory. A supernatural enemy at that.

"Please... I'm so sorry, Danny! Let me go!" he pleaded. Danny smiled, looking at him in amusement.

"Do you miss him? Your little lover boy?" Danny asked.

"You little cocksucker. Untie me now!" Keith barked, feeling powerless and enraged.

"Hmm... Now, why would I want to do that?" Danny asked calmly.

At that moment, it began to dawn on Keith that his chances of leaving Witch's Creek alive were very slim. He started jerking around violently in an attempt to free himself from the roots and vines that tied him to the tree. "You son of a bitch! Untie me now, motherfucker!"

Danny remained where he was, unmoved by his words.

Keith's attempt to break free of his bondage proved futile as the roots around him stayed tightly in place. Looking to try a different approach, he calmed himself down a bit. "You gonna kill me? Huh?" he asked in a pitiful low voice.

Danny shook his head no.

Keith was confused. If he wasn't going to kill him, then why had he dragged him into the woods? "What then?" he asked again, a glint of hope visible in his eyes.

"I won't..." Danny responded. Keith began to smile, summoning up his courage in preparation for whatever punishment awaited him; he wanted to go home. Just then, a smirk crept up the corner of Danny's mouth as he pointed and added, "I can't speak for him though."

Keith wondered what he was pointing to out of sight.

Suddenly, a large dog appeared from out of somewhere in the forest and landed right in front of him.

Scared, Keith tried to jump back but from where he was tied, all he could do was retreat further back into the tree.

Zeus's eyes glowed red as he circled around his target, calculating the right angle to pounce. Slowly, he began to take menacing steps forward, his intention obvious in his eyes.

Keith gripped the grass beneath his hands tightly, uprooting a few strands as he shuffled his legs. He began to tremble as the dog stood closely in front of him until they were face to face with each other. Zeus growled ferociously, spit flying out of his mouth. As he did, Keith noticed the dog's long canine teeth, unnaturally big, almost as if they were growing before his eyes with every growl.

Keith was stunned by fear.

At that moment, the Doberman lunged forward and brought his open mouth down on Keith's face, shaking his head vigorously until he bit off a good chunk of flesh.

Keith screamed and began thrashing frantically where he sat. Zeus dove into his deformed face again and bit his jaw off, silencing his cries.

The dog attacked him once again, his teeth sinking into his nose. Keith shook his head violently in an attempt to shake off Zeus. However, his jerking motions made it easy for the Doberman to cut his nose clean off.

Keith let out hollow screams of agony as he cursed himself for ever meeting Gill, Mitch, Jessica, and Danny. He cursed himself harder for even choosing to come into this world of endless pain.

While regrets washed over his mind, blood was flowing freely down his body. It was as if a person had open a faucet on his face while the water supply was a bloodied Nile river. His clothes were soaked with his blood, and the ground around him had turned the shade of red, with bits of meat scattered around.

Danny stood behind the dog, watching with interest as more of Keith's face was being cut off. As the Doberman moved his head lower and sank his teeth into the side of his neck, blood spurted up like a fountain, bathing the dog's darkened fur. Keith groaned and thrashed wildly, silently hoping that the dog would sever his jugular soon and send him to his peace.

───※───

The air was tense in the small conference room in the police station. Torrents of rain hit the roof of the building, making loud noises. However, none of the occupants of the room paid it much attention; they had bigger things on their collective minds.

The conference room was unusually crowded that night as Teresa, Doug, and over a dozen other officers sat around the table.

Teresa was debriefing her fellow cops on the situation at hand. She stood up and went to the board at the front of the room where several papers and photos were pinned.

"We need to contain this... whatever this is... Our suspect." She pointed to a monochrome photograph of Danny in school. "We have knowledge that a particular group of students seem to be the target, all of which were the suspect's acquaintances. Most are now dead or missing..." She pointed to another photo containing two girls with arms around each other, smiling. "Jessica and Mikayla are the only two with known locations..."

"We need two patrolmen at their location immediately," Doug stated, cutting off her statement.

Teresa shot him a warning look as she became irritated by his interruption. "No more dead bodies. No one takes a shot, unless I give the order!" she declared. The police officers nodded in understanding. "Now, suit up!" she commanded.

"Question!" an officer said, raising up to his hand. The man, Oldie Freddie, was about a decade older than Teresa. In the force, he was regarded as the most old-fashioned cop, not because of his age but due to the fact that he always took an orthodox approach to everything. Disregarding technology most times, he preferred to do the automated work by himself, which sometimes included the herculean task of filing cases. However, regardless of the man's antics, he was much respected by everyone at the police station.

Teresa nudged her head, signaling him to go ahead. "Is it true that this young man took two slugs to the chest and he's still standing?" Oldie Freddie asked.

Teresa was silent.

A younger, chatty cop, not unlike Doug, quickly fired another question at her. "What exactly are we dealing with here?"

Teresa averted her gaze and glanced sideways into the darkness outside. Just then, a bright lightning struck. Teresa counted up to six seconds, and a slight smile appeared on her face as she heard the loud rumbling noise of thunder on her last count. She turned back to face her waiting officers. "What we're facing? We are about to find out," she declared.

With that, the police officers went about suiting up for war.

———✺———

A roaring thunder shook the glass of the bedroom window. Jessica woke up with a yawn, stretching out her hands as she tried to shake her ruffled hair back in order.

After coming to, she sat up, her back propped against the headboard of the bed. The light had been turned off and the room was cast in a deep shade of darkness. However, being that Jessica had spent most of her life in this room, she was able to make out the shapes around her, even in the darkness. Beside her on the bed, she noticed Mikayla sleeping with her hands flung apart. Jessica smiled at her friend's amusing drunken sleep. After downing several shots of the whiskey, they had danced around the room until the liquor took over their systems and they fell asleep. However, that was several hours ago, she realized as she glanced at mini clock on her nightstand, pushing the little button on it for it to show the time in a digital seven segments display format.

Jessica's throat felt a little parched, and she decided to get some water. However, as she made to stand up, she found it odd that she couldn't. She tried to move her hands but she couldn't; same case for her legs; she just sat still and couldn't move any part of her body. At that moment, it dawned on her that she might be paralyzed. Was it a freaky side effect of the alcohol? She had been drunk and had experienced a hangover several times before but never to the point of paralysis. She began to freak out.

Her breath quickened as she noticed a dark figure at the corner of the room. The figure slid to the floor, and Jessica could hear it crawling on the carpeted ground toward the bed. Her heart jumped to her throat in fear. She tried to shout for help but no sound escaped her mouth. She attempted to lean over and shake Mikayla awake, but she realized she couldn't move an inch. It was as if she was rooted to the spot where she sat. The only part of her body that was moving were her eyes, which she moved around rapidly in an attempt to take in the whole scene before her.

Jessica watched as the figure climbed up the front of the bed frame and disappeared under the bed sheets. Seeing the figure up close, she realized it was more of a shadow with a girth thinner than a sheet of paper.

Jessica held her breath, hoping the figure was sightless and wouldn't be able to figure out where she was if she didn't make breathing noises. Her tactic seemed to work for a few seconds until something suddenly from beneath the sheets grabbed her by the ankle. Jessica tried to shake off the grip but she couldn't; it felt as if she was no longer in control of her body.

Slowly, the figure began to pull her under the bed sheet. Nearly all her body had gone under, with only her head remaining outside. Suddenly, she noticed the hold of the figure on her ankle was no longer there. Jessica began to heave quick, short breaths, petrified as the rest of her body was still as dead as a stone. Just then, she began to hear a ruffling noise as something began to slide beneath the sheets. She quickly rolled her eyes downward as far as they could go. Through a slit beneath the heavy clothes, she saw two tiny, shadowy legs slipping away and escaping the room through the little space below the door.

Jessica let out a long sigh, grateful that she was still alive. All she had to do now was lay still and wait for the paralysis to wear off. As she let out sighs of relief, she began to hear another scurrying noise—this time it was ten times louder and denser than before.

In fear, she waited, wondering what could be coming for her again. Just then, she began to hear the sound of hundreds of bug-like legs climbing up the wooden frame of the bed and onto the sheets. Where she played restless, unmoving, she began to feel insects walking on her legs and up her body. She put all her will power into shaking off the insects; yet still, she couldn't move.

Just then, a few of the insects began to crawl up her neck and face. She struggled to get free as she saw that the insects were big spiders the size of her thumb. Jessica was arachnophobic and as the spiders moved all over her body, she was scared out of her mind; her biggest fears were coming to reality. As if to worsen her case, the spiders on her face began to converge on a single path and they started crawling into her mouth.

Jessica shut her eyes and tried to shake her head but her effort was futile. In a last attempt to call for distress, she began to scream. Surprisingly, her voice carried loudly.

"Jessica, what's wrong?" she heard a voice call out as she felt a bright light shining down on her. Jessica opened her eyes swiftly but her eyes were caught in the direct glare of the overhead fluorescent bulb. Instantly, she closed her eyes again.

Jessica turned sideways, glad that could now move, and parted her eyelids slowly to see Mikayla's face looking down on hers. She jolted into an upright position.

"Are you okay, Jess?" Mikayla asked again, with a look of concern in her eyes.

"Yes, I'm okay. Bad dream," Jessica replied, smiling nervously. She placed her hand on her chest to calm her rapid breathing.

"No more whiskey for you, ma'am. I don't want Freddie Krueger getting you in your sleep," Mikayla said jokingly.

Jessica nodded in affirmation. "Good idea."

Mikayla smiled, finding humor in her friend's fear.

The rain continued falling heavily, making the road slippery. However, this didn't deter Danny at all as he rode his motorbike at a slow, steady pace.

His hoodie was still draped over his head, taking most of the beating of the heavy downpour. Even though water was dripping down into his eyes, he still saw clearly. Ever since he had gotten his powers from Ida, his senses had heightened, with his eyes capable of maintaining super focus while seeing from a long distance away, something no human eye could do.

Danny was thrilled by the sound of the thunder rumbling overhead. He interpreted it as a sign heralding the final phase of his vengeance. As he rode on, he thought back to the event that occurred earlier in the day. He knew if Zeus could talk, the dog would've thanked him graciously for blessing him with such as huge supper. If anybody dared to venture into Witch's Creek in search of

Keith, all they would find were pieces of ripped clothes and a few splintered bones that the Doberman considered too small to swallow. Danny smiled as he reminisced on the fine details of the scene.

As he rode his bike on in a jolly spirit, he spotted light coming from a section in Jessica's house a short distance ahead. Danny pulled off the road and parked his bicycle in the nearby forest. He decided to walk the rest of the distance to the house. He didn't want to spook them with the sound of the automobile.

Danny began to approach the house. He whistled heartily as he went, unbothered by the rain thrashing him.

Oliver stood by the window, peering out into the night. The beautiful, full length window stretched from the floor to the ceiling. From Oliver's standing point, the only thing he could see outside was the thick forest, which was currently being heavily thrashed by the downpour of rain.

From somewhere behind him, he heard the soft beep of the cooking counter, signaling that his cooking was done. He quickly turned around from the window and hurried into the kitchen.

Jessica rubbed her eyes, trying to banish away sleep as she dreaded having another freakish nightmare. In order to keep her mind preoccupied, she sat at the edge of her bed with a box of relics from her past laid beside her. The box contained pictures, drawings, toys, and other items she had held dear before she marked her first decade on Earth. The box had been locked inside the bottom shelf of her cupboard for a long time and it had been many years since she'd touched it, the proof being the fair amount of dust that had gathered on the carton.

Jessica had been whipped into a tumultuous, unstable, and dangerous world lately. She was about to lose her mind in fright, and in order to keep her sanity, she had decided to revisit her past, to find a semblance of peace and happiness. As Jessica went through the items in the box, nostalgia crept up into her mind. She noticed a doll at the corner of the box. "Oh, Bixby!" she exclaimed excitedly as she pulled out the doll and held it to her chest. She smiled, remembering how much fun she had had playing with the doll whenever she got back home from school. Now, as she stared at the doll, she noticed it had lost an arm, its clothes were tattered, and its hair was ragged and cut in several places. "You don't look much worse than me," she muttered, chuckling.

She patted the doll on the head lightly and made to return it to its abode in the carton. However, as she stretched out her hand to place it in, she saw something in the box that made her heart jump. Lying above a collection of photos was a picture of Jessica and Danny, with arms across each other's backs. Reflexively, her hand went to her mouth, muffling a gasp as her eyes widened. Slowly, she pulled out the photo and stared at the bright smile on their little faces, set in the grayscale background. When Jessica had brought out the box, she had known there was a great chance that she would come across something that tied them together in the past as they had spent a lot of time together growing up. However, she hadn't expected that it would be so overwhelming. Seeing their hearty smiles, the innocence in their faces, and how happy they were in each other's company then brought her near to tears.

Jessica sniffled as she returned the photo. She couldn't bring herself to look at more items from her past so she closed the box and placed it back into the corner. She couldn't prevent the tear that dropped from her eye.

Just then, her father shouted from the kitchen, "Ask Mikayla what she wants, chicken or pork?"

Even though he shouted, his voice was barely loud enough to reach the room over the noise of the rumbling thunder.

Jessica hadn't heard her father's question as her mind was elsewhere. However, Mikayla had heard and she replied for herself with a louder shout, "Chicken please!" She hoped her yelled had been loud enough as she felt so stressed out and couldn't bring herself to stand up and go to the kitchen.

Luckily for her, Oliver had heard her response and he went about making the preparations. At that moment, lightning struck outside, making him jolt in shock as he opened up a cabinet. "Dammit!" he cussed, as he couldn't find what he was searching for.

He went into the pantry, flicking on the light as he stepped inside. The bulb shone brightly, illuminating the small room. However, as Oliver headed toward the shelves, the light bulb fizzled out unexpectedly. "Oh, really...?" he muttered in exasperation.

He went down on his knees and opened the bottom cabinet, looking through cans. In the darkness, his elbow accidentally knocked it over, making a clattering sound as it hit the ground. "Shit!" he muttered.

The can began to roll slowly out of the pantry and into the kitchen. At first, Oliver couldn't tell where it was. However, as he saw it roll into the living room den, he followed his basic instinct, which was to crawl after it.

The can gained momentum as it reached a slightly elevated slope and stopped into a pair of boots just in front of him. Oliver stopped proceeding instantly as fear gripped him. Slowly, he looked up to see a tall, dark figure in the dimly lit room. He jumped back, scared as he quickly ran to turn on the lights, with the figure still glaring at him, unmoving.

When the lights came on, Oliver couldn't help but laugh as he saw that what he had been so scared of was only a coat and boots on a hook. "Bitch ass," he said to himself as he shook his head, laughing.

He rubbed his elbow that was beginning to hurt as he went over to pick the can. He was feeling tense already, and he knew whenever he got that way, his mind would be jumbled up. He needed something to calm himself and with booze not being an option, the answer was music.

Placing the can on the kitchen counter, he walked over to the stereo system in the living room and turned it on, tweaking its controls a little bit. A few seconds later, the sound system began to belt out Dean Martin's song, *Sway.*

Oliver took a deep breath, sighing loudly as he was beginning to feel the soothing effect of the music already. He swayed slowly as he went back into the kitchen to resume his cooking.

Lightning struck again, illuminating the surroundings of the house, but Oliver couldn't be bothered to turn around to look this time as he was in the spirit of the melody already; he whistled along to the tune and gyrated his body as he prepared the gravy for their meal.

At that moment, a figure shrouded in black from head to toe stood outside the window where Jessica's father had just left a few minutes earlier. The figure peered into the house, watching the man dancing like he had won the lottery. A crooked smile crept up the figure's face.

"Move it, move it!" Officer Teresa barked at the cops as they loaded their weapons. "Yes, ma'am!" they chorused.

"A second can't be wasted, get your behinds out now!"

This seemed to motivate the officers as they hurried out into the waiting squad cars, not minding the rain that sent chills into their bodies.

Soon, five police cars began to barrel down the road, headed toward the potential victim's residence. Teresa rode in the lead car, along with a SWAT unit. As the rains splattered on the windshield angrily, she said a silent prayer that they would be able to get to Jessica's house on time. She was aware of the bond between Jessica and Danny and she knew if he harmed her, he would be well past the point of redemption.

"C'mon, c'mon!" She willed the squad car to go faster as she tapped her foot on the floor in agitation.

———

Sway still played on the stereo, however, louder as Oliver had cranked up the volume when he went to put the song on repeat. Now, back in the kitchen, chopping vegetables, he danced with more vigor, sometimes putting down the knife just to snap his fingers to the rhythm.

At that moment, a black, thick liquid with the appearance of coal tar began to flow into the house from under the front door. The thick, viscous liquid began to flow slowly toward the kitchen as if it had a mind of its own.

Oliver swayed his hips like *Magic Mike* giving himself a good and energetic solo performance. As he made to rotate his hips, the music stopped abruptly. Oliver was irritated by this and he quickly whirled around, thinking it was his daughter that had hindered his private show. However, he was surprised to see that there was no one around.

He marched over to the stereo and pushed a few buttons; nothing happened. Oliver was puzzled as he wondered if the lightning had affected the electrical appliances in the house. He crouched and leaned forward to give the stereo a closer look.

Just then, he noticed the black liquid on the carpeted floor. "What the hell?" he muttered as he made to inspect it. To his utmost surprise, the still liquid began to flow sideways. Oliver jumped back, falling on his ass and scampering up quickly as he retracted into the hall.

Surprisingly, rather than the liquid coming after him, it retracted back into the darkness before completely dissipating. Oliver began to shiver not due to the cold weather but as a result of the crippling fear in his heart. He couldn't call out for help as he knew that would be putting the girls into perpetual danger, if there was one.

His fears were confirmed when he looked into the corner of the room and saw a pair of eyes staring at him from the darkness. Oliver held his breath, afraid that the figure would be able to sense his fears through his hyperventilation. Just then, he couldn't help but see the set of teeth that broke into a maniacal grin as it was the only whiteness coming from the darkness.

Oliver heard a sound of raspy exhaling, which made him cower in fear where he stood. With the evilness that the entity exuded, Oliver knew there was no escape for him—he couldn't outrun the darkness. He finally let out a long sigh and silently prayed for his soul as the figure stepped out of the darkness and began to approach him.

Mikayla jumped off the bed, the foot of her slippers landing on the floor with a soft thud. Her spirits were getting elevated already as her fears dissipated in the company of her friend. "I'm going to grab a bottle of water, want one?"

Jessica nodded. "Yeah, they're in the pantry."

Mikayla headed out of the room and climbed down the stairs that led to the hallway. Smoke filled the air, accompanied by the scent of burning food. "Master Chef burning dinner?" she teased. Hearing no response, she decided to check the kitchen. To her surprise, the food on the stove was badly burnt as it had nearly completely blackened. Smoke filled Mikayla's lungs as she leaned down to turn off the stove. She quickly went over to the wall and pushed the switch that turned on the overhead kitchen fan.

As she looked around at the messy kitchen, she wondered where Jessica's father had gone, carelessly leaving the food he was cooking. The smoke that still hung and the air stung her eyes as she walked around. "Mr. O?" she called out as she waved the smoke, coughing as she spoke.

No response still.

The only sounds she could hear were that of the still sizzling pot and that of the TV static coming from the living room. She rolled her eyes. Jessica's dad had probably dozed off while watching the television, she thought.

Mikayla headed into the dark living room and grabbed the TV remote. She pushed the mute button while the screen still remained on static, providing the only illumination in the room. The light wasn't sufficient enough to reach more than a few inches radius, and the rest of the room was engulfed in darkness.

She tossed the remote onto a couch ahead and was surprised to hear it landing on a person's body with a soft thud. "Mr. O?" she said as she began to approach, ready to apologize for throwing the remote at him.

"I'm really sorry, I had no idea," she called out as she got nearer.

There was no response, and the person just sat there with his head bent downward as if in meditation.

The hair on Mikayla's arms sprang up as she began to get nervous. Why was Jessica's father ignoring her?

As she stood right in front of him, she strained her eyes in the darkness to see whether the man was praying. Just then, with his head still bent low, he stretched out his hand and began to extend it toward her.

"What's that, sir?" Mikayla asked, confused as she began to get freaked out. She glared at him more intently and noticed that his hand was darker than usual, with thick lines running all over it; realization dawned on her at that moment.

Just then, Danny raised his head and stretched it out for her to see in the light. "Boo," he shouted.

Mikayla screamed as she turned around and bolted toward the kitchen. Danny sprang up but before his hands could clasp around her, she was out of his grasp.

He began to chase after her but in his excitement, he didn't concentrate, and he slammed into a chair, knocking it over.

Mikayla ran into the kitchen and picked up the knife on the island, wiping the vegetables on its blade off on her shirt.

By then, Danny was already close to the kitchen and seeing Mikayla ahead with a knife in hand, he got himself off the floor and began to walk to her, taking his time.

With each step he took, Mikayla retreated. However, as he got closer to her, she had run her back into the wall. Seeing there was nowhere to back into anymore, she ran around the kitchen island, with Danny chasing after her.

They did this for a while, and when Danny couldn't catch up with her, he stopped. By then, she was standing at the opposite side of the island.

"Stay back," Mikayla warned, holding the knife in front of her.

Danny smiled, looking at her with amusement in his eyes. "Or what?" he said. He began to take slow steps toward her.

"I said get the fuck back!" Mikayla yelled, trying to exude bravery, but the knife in her shaky hands betrayed her confidence as she took a few retreating steps.

By then, they had gone in another full cycle, and Danny's back was now to the living room. "Okay... you win," he stated as he raised his hands up above his head in surrender. However, rather than walk toward her, he took a few steps back into the shadows and disappeared into the darkness.

Mikayla stood rooted to the spot she was for a few seconds, her shaky hands still gripping the knife, wondering where he had gone. After a long minute of waiting, all the time dreading his reemergence, he didn't come out of the shadows, and Mikayla took the opportunity to escape as she backed away slowly toward the stairs, her eyes still darting around, expecting Danny to spring out of living room. Each second of his disappearance made her more worried as she kept wondering what evil plans he had in mind for her.

Mikayla trembled as she was nearly paralyzed by dread. Her eyes keep raving around the kitchen in hopes and fears of seeing him.

Just then, a slight shadow appeared behind her and out of it jumped Danny. Before she could turn around, a hand grabbed her mouth and body, dragging her into the darkness.

Jessica was startled by a loud thump that came from downstairs. She quickly ran out and stood in the stairway. "Dad?" she called out.

There was a scuffling noise coming from just beneath the stairs. Slowly, Jessica began to climb down, her neck craned in anticipation. As she stepped down the last stair, there was no one in sight, but the noises she was hearing had grown much louder.

She quickened her pace as she entered the kitchen where the noise was originating from. Her jaw dropped in shock at the sight before her. Mikayla was trying to scream, but the sounds coming from her lungs couldn't escape as Danny's hand was over her mouth.

"Shhhh," Danny was whispering into Mikayla's ears. His other hand was on her neck, crushing her throat slowly. Jessica's intrusion had little effect on his resolve as he maintained his grip on Mikayla's throat.

Jessica was dumbstruck for a second as she watched Danny suffocate her friend. It felt surreal, like she was in a trance. However, as she heard the sound of crunching bones, she snapped back into reality. "Please, Danny... Stop..." she screamed.

"No," Danny stated simply as he tightened his grip.

Mikayla began to gasp as the air supply was completely cut from her lungs. She stretched out her hand toward Jessica as her eyes reddened. She wanted to scream out in pain and cry but, she was denied both privileges.

Jessica was horrified as the sound of breaking bones grew louder as Danny squeezed Mikayla's neck like an empty can of soda. Mikayla's body began to go limp as her hand flapped and fell beside her.

Danny was expressionless as he felt the life go out of her eyes. He slowly removed his hands from around her neck, and all he felt was satisfaction as he watched her body crumple onto the floor like a rag doll, with her hands flailed out and her lustrous, long, black hair spread across the floor.

Jessica cried out in horror as Danny murdered her friend right in front of her eyes. She felt sorrow like never before in her life. This had gone much farther than she could have ever imagined. She was sickened by the violence, and she prayed that it would end there.

Just then, Danny turned to her. In his black eyes was a very glaring message: *You are next!*

Jessica didn't wait a single moment longer before she turned around and ran toward the front door, her neck craned backward, watching Danny chase after her as she pulled open the door and jumped outside.

As she stepped onto the front porch, she was greeted by a growling noise. Instantly, Jessica stopped running as she came face to face with Zeus. The Doberman's bark was loud enough to wake a whole town as his mouth opened wide, with long fangs glistening under the moonlight. Saliva dripped from the corner of his hungry mouth, and with each ferocious bark, saliva flew out of his mouth, bathing Jessica.

Jessica glanced back and saw Danny at the end of the dark hall, walking slowly toward her. She knew she was caught between a rock and a hard place, with each one meaning certain death for her. She knew there was no negotiating with the dog, but she hoped there was still an iota of compassion in whatever had possessed Danny.

With that, she made her decision, stepping back slowly into the house. She was scared out of her senses and in her jittery state, her legs hooked each other and she tripped.

Seeing her lying on the ground, Danny lunged at her, covering the distance between them until his shadow was looming over her. Her stared down at her, his shrouded figure giving him the appearance of the grim reaper, ready to harvest her soul and send her to Tartarus.

"Danny, please… I didn't know… It wasn't me…" she sobbed as she slowly got up to her feet, wondering why he hadn't snuffed the life out of her yet.

Something stirred deep inside Danny as a childhood memory flashed in his mind. He hesitated for a second, his menacing demeanor softening.

Jessica noticed the shift in him as she cried; in the darkness, she could have sworn that she saw a little light in his eyes. She silently hoped that she had gotten through to him.

As she made to continue talking, Danny clenched his jaws and looked into her eyes, his soul laid bare and emotionless. His eyeballs had grown fully dark again, and the veins on his face were now thicker and more prominent than before. He began to reach his hand out toward her neck.

Just then, the squad cars pulled up in front of the house, and Teresa was the first to jump out and began running toward the house.

Danny heard the nuisance, but he didn't throw the cops a single glance as he knew there was practically nothing they could do to stop him from exerting his revenge.

As his hand nearly closed around Jessica's neck, Teresa climbed up the porch and seeing what he was about to do through the open door, shouted, "Danny! Don't move!" She raised her gun.

The sound of her familiar voice left Danny momentarily dazed, drawing his attention.

He stopped reaching for Jessica and turned his head sideways to look at his ex-lover.

Teresa still pointed the gun at him, even though the dog was a few meters away from her. For some reason, the dog stopped barking as it saw her, instead, watching her with wary eyes. "Jessica, get in my car... now!" Teresa ordered.

Jessica quickly stepped out through the door, taking slow steps as she maneuvered around the dog. As she was able to get past the porch successfully, she ran the rest of the way toward the cop cars as the rain thrashed her head mercilessly.

Meanwhile, Teresa stepped around the dog and walked into the house, approaching Danny with caution. She noticed the change in Danny as he stepped back into the shadows, disappearing. She followed after him.

At that moment, Doug was leading a small unit of five police officers around the house. He raised his fist up with his palms clenched. The train of officers behind him stopped immediately at his signal.

Teresa navigated through the darkness, peering out for him. "Look at me. We can fix this, this isn't you. We can live together, just us," she called to him. To prove the how genuine her words were, she lowered her weapon and stood straight, beckoning him to come out.

As if by command, Danny lowered his guard and stepped out of the darkness, approaching Teresa with caution. As he stood before her, Teresa wasn't scared or terrified by his appearance; rather, all she felt for him was compassion. She closed the gap between them and placed her hands on his shoulders.

At her touch, his shoulders slumped, and he seemed to relax. His menacing facial expression softened, and the veins on his face became less prominent.

"Come with me, Danny," Teresa said affectionately as she began to lead him by the shoulders toward the front door.

Danny followed her without questions, his feet dragging against the floor as he stepped outside onto the porch.

It was still raining all around, but its intensity had reduced and the lightning and thunder had nearly stopped altogether.

Danny and Teresa just stood there on the porch and all they were doing was staring into each other's eyes.

Meanwhile, Doug had taken position as he peeked out from the corner of the house, he and his men with their guns ready. He was surprised and confused to see Teresa standing so close to the murderous boy and touching him. He couldn't hear what they were saying over the sound of the rain so he decided to get closer and listen. As he lifted his boot, his eyes were still trained on the couple in front of the house. He didn't look as he brought his leg down on a metal plate, sending noise echoing into the night.

Danny became alerted as he shot Doug a sideways glance. The police officer shook in fear. Spooked, he fired a shot at Danny. Instantly, Danny pushed Teresa away as more officers began to fire at him from various directions.

Several bullets hit Danny, rocking his body where he stood.

Teresa was only a few meters away from him and she was annoyed by what was happening. "Hold your fi—" The last word stuck in her as a bullet ricocheted off Danny and nailed her in the neck.

Instantly, Danny turned his direction to her and caught her before she hit the ground.

Swiftly, he turned his back to the cops as swarms of bullets pelted him.

Teresa's head was cushioned in his arm as her dizzy eyes glared up at him. Danny's clothes had been ripped into holes in several places as the bullets still rained down on his back. He didn't pay them much attention as he was focused on the woman who lay in his arms, dying.

Teresa coughed up blood, spilling some onto Danny's sleeves as her breath quickened.

For the first time since his transformation, Danny felt completely human. He felt like his former self, lost and confused as sorrow washed over him. "Teresa…" he muttered, saddened.

10

NO MORE

The tire of the truck was spinning slowly with no friction to stop it as it stuck up in the air. Inside the upturned truck, little Danny crawled out through its broken window. He looked around, his seven-year-old brain not fully comprehending the full implication of what had just happened as he looked at the badly damaged truck.

With his teddy bear in hand, Danny began to walk toward where his mother had flown out to earlier.

"Danny! Hey! Stop!" his father called out. David was pinned between the dashboard and his chair and he found it hard to move. He reached out his hand to grab Danny but couldn't. "Danny!" he yelled as he saw his little boy still walking toward where Elinore lay, probably dead. He didn't want his son to see such a sight, let alone know the person who did. He began to wriggle where he was hooked, trying

to free his shoulders. However, he was unsuccessful, and each movement he made caused him intense pain.

Danny saw his mother sprawled out on the ground beneath a tall tree, her body contorted in an odd shape. He dropped his doll and began to walk toward her slowly. Standing in front of her, he started to say, "Mommy... Wake up, Mommy, wake up!"

A bullet hit Danny in the neck, snapping him back from his reverie. He realized he just came back from one disheartening nightmare to another as he looked down to see Teresa gargling blood. Just then, their eyes made contact one last time before her head dropped as she gave up the ghost.

As Danny watched the person he cared about the most die, his feelings instantly changed from sorrow and pain to anger, hatred, and rage. He dropped Teresa's body on the floor and slammed his fist down, breaking the wooden floorboard before hitting the ground.

Seeing his display of anger, the police officers stopped shooting.

The whole world went silent for several seconds. Then, roots and vines shot out from the forest, grabbing the officers by their feet and waists before dragging them into the forest, which was pitch black that night. The roots wound tightly around them before shooting through their bodies, piercing their eyes, mouths, and chests. Of the whole squad of police that got pulled into the forest, the only things that came out from the woods were their screams, which quickly became muffled as tree branches twisted, snapping the necks of the cops.

Back at the house, Danny lifted Teresa's body from the ground and began to walk toward the forest. He paid no attention to the rest of the officers who were being dragged into the dark forest as they tried to make a run for it.

Throughout the whole encounter, Jessica had knelt beside one of the police cars and had kept her head low. After the fight had subsided and no police officer was left standing again, Jessica stuck her head out, looking around in hopes that she wouldn't get dragged into the forest like the unfortunate souls who had come to her rescue. She waited for a few seconds and seeing that she was relatively safe, she stepped out of her hiding place.

The night's events had drawn out for long and Jessica had no idea how long it was until she looked up and saw the rising sun. The red hue of the large ball of fire seemed deeper than usual, and Jessica believed that the rich crimson color of the sun that day was because of the blood that had been spilled at her house overnight.

Heavy footsteps jolted her back to the present and she looked ahead and saw Danny disappearing into the forest with Teresa's body in his arms. Jessica began to hurry after him. The logical parts of her brain had grown numb, and she couldn't stop her legs from moving even if she tried as the inquisitive spirit in her had taken over already. She didn't have much to hold on to anymore, she figured. Her life was worth very little at that moment after the carnage she had just witnessed at her home, which had taken the lives of servicemen and her best friend. As she stepped into the forest, she presumed that her father's body was also very likely lying around somewhere in the large, soulless house. She wondered if she should go check if he was still alive. However, she couldn't bring herself to find out yet. There was comfort in the uncertainty.

Ahead, Danny set Teresa down against an obnoxiously large tree. Teresa was unmoving, dead, with dried blood all over her face and clothes.

Jessica hid behind a cluster of short shrubs, her head peeking out slightly as she watched from a distance. She tried to control her breathing in order to ensure she wasn't sounding too loud to spook him. After her experience over the night, she would hate to be the person that pisses him off while he was trying to mourn his lover. She wondered what sort of bond existed between the unlikely pair that Teresa would put her life on the line for him, ending up losing it, and why Danny would go to such lengths to shield her and get revenge on the unfortunate policemen who had killed her. The image of the servicemen contorted in grotesque shapes was permanently seared into her head and lest she dip a sponge in vinegar and washed her brain with it, she knew she would be scarred forever. Although, that forever seemed to have a bleak future from where she was positioned.

Danny stood over Teresa's body and stretched out his hands, placing one on Teresa's throat wound and the other on the large tree. He channeled some energy from the earth and into her lifeless body. He looked up, and relief washed over him as the tree began to dry up while color was beginning to rush back into her body.

As the tree withered completely, he removed his hand from Teresa's neck and was unsurprised to see that the entry wound of the bullet had sealed up with no scars on the spot.

Jessica nearly tumbled into the bush when she saw Teresa take a deep breath. Although, still laid where she was, probably unconscious, Teresa was alive and breathing well.

Just then, Danny slowly kissed Teresa's forehead. He turned his head around, staring at a petrified Jessica in the eyes before he began to head into the darkest and deepest part of the forest.

11

STATIC

Beside the welcome sign to Sherbrooke is a spot where Officer Rick liked to sit. Shaded on both sides by trees and waist-high foliage, he had the advantage of staying out of sight while observing the highway for traffic offenders. The tall trees of Sherbrooke forest cast long shadows that danced across the asphalt, their movement —like the sullen face of the sky — was an anomaly. There was no wind, and the officer wondered what caused them to sway. No sound was heard except the call of the wolves coming from the depths of the forest. They usually roamed in packs amongst the distant mountains. Now and then they were sighted at the edges of the forest prancing amongst the trees.

He gently adjusted the mirror on his police motorcycle, turning it this way and that when a sudden whoosh of air threw him off balance. For a hot second, he stopped and all the rookie officer could see through his blurred vision was a cloud of gray dust running forward on the lonely Sherbrooke road. The rains came with a vengeance at the heels of the gray dust, slamming into the earth at an angle that had the young officer wondering whether the gods were throwing stones. He caught himself leaning too far to the left of his motorbike.

"What the hell…" the young officer swore under his breath while throwing out a leg to balance himself back on his bike. He threw it into gear and slammed on his siren in one swift movement, going out quickly after whatever it was that had raised such disturbance. As he accelerated, small beads of rain hit his bike slowly but surely, soaking him. He found that the rain seemed to intensify as he closed in on the car. The wail of an engine at its maximum speed could be heard faintly over the sound of his motorbike's sirens as he closed the gap. He noticed the car slowing down and decelerated with his mind still befuddled as to where such abrupt rain had come from. He parked a few steps behind the black vehicle and began to walk gently toward it; he could make it out now: a 1969 Camaro SS with the engine still running. While he walked, Officer Rick was on high alert and kept his eyes peeled. He wiped his visor now, finding that he was suddenly sweating even with the rainwater cascading down his face. Something was wrong here and he wondered what it could be. His senses were heightened and he could feel the beating of his heart slightly accelerate as he noticed the tight grip of the hand holding the steering wheel of the black Camaro.

"Bark!" came the sound from the back seat, and Officer Rick jumped, the sudden noise adding to the weariness he already felt. He jumped too quickly, his heart thumping in his chest as a massive 18 wheeler closed in, running very close to the parked Camaro. Officer Rick wouldn't have made it no matter how fast he was, but then he felt a hand grab and pull him clear of the speeding 18 wheeler truck which would have surely made a mush of his body just then. He held his heart which was threatening to pull out of its ribcage. It was clear to him at that moment whatever was in that car had just saved his skin from certain death. He stood a while, staring at the truck that nearly ended his life only moments ago. The hand that had saved him was still holding onto his belt from an angle. It slowly released him, and Officer Rick breathed deeply, trying to steady his breath. He turned back to the occupants of the car…

"krrrrrr… krrrrr," came the static off Officer Rick's radio.

He jumped but quickly gained his composure and pulled the radio off its place on his shoulder, bringing it up to his ears.

"krrrrr suspect heading north… krrrrr… black…"

Officer Rick quickly replaced his shoulder walkie and swallowed hard. His steps weren't as sure as they used to be. He walked toward the passenger side of the vehicle with his hand on the butt of the Glock 22 sitting on his belt holster. He thought he had managed to get the rapid thump of his heartbeat under control but he realized now that he hadn't. He could still hear the heaviness in his ears.

"Do you know how fast you were going?"

"Fast…" the driver of the Camaro began to say when the walkie went off again.

"…suspect is highly dangerous… krrrr… Chevy… krrrr…" The walkie went off completely now, leaving the fragments it coughed up echoing in the tall trees. The officer turned back to the occupants of the car. He had no doubt the suspect being announced over the radio could be the one standing before him. He gauged his ability to take him in. Rick could see the set eyes of the driver; he wore an intense stare that bore straight down the road and did not make eye contact.

"I would like you to step out of the vehi…" Before he could finish the sentence, Officer Rick noticed the hand on the steering wheel tightening. The veins on them were bulging visibly and were beginning to turn black. The blacker the veins became the heavier the downpour seemed to be. Officer Rick did a double take, looking back and forth for signs of his colleagues. Nothing. The rookie officer swallowed the lump that had suddenly appeared and wiped the liquid hanging on his brows.

"Erm, I think I will let you off with a warning this time."

Before he could finish, the tires of the Camaro tore into the asphalt. Officer Rick could smell the result of the friction. As he watched the car drive off, he quickly heard growls; the sound was more intense than that which he had heard earlier. He turned and stared back for a minute at the forest. The sound of wolves came hard and hot, increasing with tempo at each howl. It magnified, now coming from all sides yet confined among the trees of the forest. Officer Rick pulled out his gun, frantically looking around but noticing the wolves howling among the trees made no move to enter the clear road, almost as if they couldn't. He turned and watched the Camaro race into the distant stretch of road, noticing the wolf pack following. He felt the rain stop abruptly. He raised his head up to the sky wondering if a tarp had been thrown over his head, but there was nothing. All that was left were clear skies.

ABOUT THE AUTHOR

Born and raised in the Windy City, Daniel Sacketos is an actor, entrepreneur, and now author. His early love for fiction and especially horror led him to write his first novel Darkened. Daniel spent countless hours as a child devouring as many horror novels and movies as he could find. Like any good author, Daniel attributes his drive to reading and his love for film.

When not writing, Daniel enjoys spending time with family, being outdoors, and traveling around the world.

To discover more about Daniel and his unique brand of storytelling, you can follow him on Instagram @dsacketos

For exclusive perks and to support author visit https://www.patreon.com/Dannywrites123

CPSIA information can be obtained
at www.ICGtesting.com
Printed in the USA
LVHW091040300420
654780LV00007B/84